W9-BCD-433
3 1230 00852 2910

Stealth

The Urbana Free Library

DISCARDED BY THE
URBANA FREE LIBRARY

To renew: call 217-367-4057
or go to "*urbanafreelibrary.org*"
and select "Renew/Request Items"

Also by Sonallah Ibrahim

AVAILABLE FROM NEW DIRECTIONS

That Smell & Notes from Prison

Stealth

Sonallah Ibrahim

Translated from the Arabic by
Hosam Aboul-Ela

A NEW DIRECTIONS BOOK

Copyright © 2007 by Sonallah Ibrahim
Translation copyright © 2009, 2014 by Hosam Aboul-Ela

All rights reserved. Except for brief passages quoted in a newspaper, magazine,
radio, television, or website review, no part of this book may be reproduced
in any form or by any means, electronic or mechanical, including
photocopying and recording, or by any information storage and retrieval
system, without permission in writing from the Publisher.

First published in Arabic as *Al Talassus* by Dar al-Mustaqbil al-Arabi in 2007.

Manufactured in the United States of America
New Directions Books are printed on acid-free paper
First published as a New Directions Paperbook (NDP1293) in 2014
Design by Erik Rieselbach

Library of Congress Cataloging-in-Publication Data
Ibrahim, Sun' Allah.
[Talassus. English]
Stealth / Sonallah Ibrahim ;
translated from the Arabic by Hosam Aboul-Ela.
pages cm
ISBN 978-0-8112-2305-8 (pbk. : alk. paper)
1. Fathers and sons—Egypt—Cairo—Fiction.
2. Cairo (Egypt)—Social life and customs—Fiction.
I. Aboul-Ela, Hosam M., translator.
II. Title.
PJ7838.B7173T3513 2014
892.736—dc23
2013049759

1 3 5 7 9 10 8 6 4 2

ndbooks.com

New Directions Books are published for James Laughlin
by New Directions Publishing Corporation
80 Eighth Avenue, New York 10011

Stealth

Chapter One

My father stops for a second at the door to the house before we step into the alley. He raises his hand to his mouth, twisting the curved ends of his grey moustache upwards. He makes sure that his fez tilts slightly to the left. He removes the black, burnt-out cigarette from the corner of his mouth. Brushes off ash that has dropped on to the front of his thick black overcoat. He wipes his face to smooth the wrinkles in his forehead and forces a smile across his lips. He grabs hold of my left hand. We feel our way forward in the light of the sunset.

We head towards the right, the only way out of our alley, picking our way to the winding main street with its crowds of people and shops. At the market, Hajj Abdel 'Alim, the sheikh of the quarter, calls to us from his shop: "Please, stop in for a while, Khalil Bey."

My father answers him quietly: "We'll pass by on our way back."

The chemist. His shop is clean and gives off a smell of phenol. A glass bowl is piled high with chocolates and sweets. I pull my father's hand towards it and he scolds me.

The shoe shop. A shoeshine man sits at the bottom of a

raised chair. A newspaper rack stands in front and a huge radio at the back.

The fez press. It has a long brass base and a big brass molding on top.

Then finally, the square.

Its light is pale in the first few minutes of evening. The picture of the king is lit by lamps. Posters congratulate him on his birthday. Billboards for cinemas. The film *Hassan the Brave* is playing in living color. *The Black Knight* is playing at Cinema Miami, with Arabic subtitles. I feel a cool breeze slapping at my bare knees between the bottoms of my shorts and the tops of my long woolen socks. My left hand feels warm in my father's strong grip. Tram number 22 with its open cars and wooden benches. *I race beside the tramcar with the children running along its left side. I jump on it at the last second to show we can escape the ticket collector, almost falling underneath its rows of metal wheels.*

We board the second car, and he squeezes me down in the corner so I'll look younger than I am. He pulls eight millimes out of his breast pocket for the ticket. We get off at Sayyida Square, flooded with lights. The Swaris bus is pulled by two skinny mules. Its passengers fill out its benches facing each other and spilling on to its back steps. The driver's whip lashes across the backs of the two animals. An old, fat woman squats on the floor around a tray of cigarette butts. In a cramped space at the end there is a small desk behind a glass partition. An old, hunchbacked man with a thick beard. My father takes his round pocket watch out of his breast pocket. The old man eyes it carefully until he puts it aside and puts down his money.

Again, the busy street. The lottery seller hangs his tickets on the wall. My father takes out two tickets and his reading glasses. He compares his numbers to the register of the seller. He tears up the two tickets and throws them aside. He buys two new tickets, a red one and a blue one.

A row of hawkers selling used goods, and shoeshiners. A stack of old eyeglasses on a newspaper on the ground. The salesman wears prescription glasses with a broken bridge in the middle, soldered together with a big piece of tin. My father bends over and shuffles through the glasses. He chooses one and asks me to try them on. I put the glasses over my eyes and look around. I try another pair. A third pair has thin, oval frames made from gilded metal. I can tell that my vision is better now. Father haggles for a while over the price then buys them.

I put the glasses on and follow father to the spice shop.

He buys cinnamon, crushed black pepper, and cloves. I can see clearly now.

Again, we take the tram with the open car. We go to the back and ride the covered car at the end with the single bench facing backwards. We shoot like an arrow past the empty stations that no riders have asked for. Sparks flick off the contact pole. I put my hand over my glasses, scared that they might fly off. We rumble slowly into Al-Zahir Square. The open-air Cinema Valery has closed for winter. *My mother is in a colored dress. Her head is covered by a silk sash that wraps around her face. Her shoes are blue and white. They have a medium high heel and closed toe. She sits in a chair with wicker arms. I try to sit on her lap but she pushes me away. My father takes me between his knees. A hawker passes by wearing a clean gallabiya and carrying a basket covered with a cloth.*

My father buys each of us a sameet, a pretzel with sesame seeds. The hawker gives us each a slice of Egyptian Romano cheese in a bite-sized wrapper.

The covered car rocks back and forth. My father pulls me to him to protect me from the cold wind. I shrink into his hug. His odor of stale tobacco swallows me. I fight off drowsiness. I feel an urge to get up and turn the brake arm, just to see what happens to the wheel on the tracks. I wish I could be in bed already. *I am on a mat stretched over a rug in the guest room next to the servant woman. The room is dark and the door is cracked open just enough to see through to the hall. There is a ray of light from the electric lamp in the dining room. The servant sings along with the radio: "Oh, your coal black eyes . . ." Her soft voice whispers next to my ear. Her hand plays with my hair and touches my head. She finishes the song and tells me the story of Hassan the Brave. In the darkness, the seats turn into mountains, stallions, and castles. Hassan the Brave suckles at the breast of a ghoul, who says to him: "You took a little milk from my right breast and became like my child Sama'ain, and you took a little milk from my left breast and became like my child Soleiman."*

The tram slows as it approaches the square. We get off and cross back over the track. Father stops at the butcher's. He has a huge frame and fine dark black moustache. He wears a white *gallabiya* dappled with spots of blood. Father asks for a pound of boneless meat that will make a good *kamuniyya* stew.

The butcher rolls up the sleeves of his *gallabiya* to show a wool undershirt that is sort of beige-colored. He looks over the different chunks of meat hanging on the hooks. He grabs one of them. He throws it on to a round wooden chopping block and rains blows down on it with a wide cleaver. Then he switches to a short knife to cut the meat off the bone. He lifts a piece of the meat up in the air in front of our eyes. Father asks him to trim off the fat and gristle. He puts the piece on to the scale of the brass measure. He moves it to the chopping block and grabs a long knife with a shiny blade. He cuts it into evenly sized pieces.

Father asks him about the health of his father, Mu'alim Nasehy, and says he has not seen him in a while. The butcher avoids my father's stare as he says: "Fine, praise God."

I sneak away from my father and move around the chopping block. The butcher moves the meat away from its edge. He takes it and starts to roll it into thick, grey wrapping paper. He pushes at a piece until it drops on the ground, then he leaves it there. I want to make father see it, but when he takes up the roll I follow him out of the shop.

I let him know what I saw. He laughs and says it is just the way butchers are. There is no hope for them. He has to be happy just being able to find the cut he wants. He says that he has been dealing with the butcher's father for twenty years. He would make special trips to see him from the house in Al-Barad Street where Nabila was born.

We head towards the dairy shop. We buy two dishes of *mehlabbiya* for dessert. We cross the square again. We pause in front of a cart with a tall pile of green *ful* beans. Father asks how much they cost. He buys a pound. We head towards our street. The chemist is closed and my father says that he usually closes around *al-'ash'a*, the last prayer of the day.

We enter Hajj Abdel 'Alim's shop and find him at a desk in the back, sitting under a big picture of the king. He looks skinny in his thick brown overcoat over his woolen robe. There's a white *kaffiyeh* around his neck and he is wearing a fez. He lets out a choppy cough every few minutes. He pushes to his feet to greet father. Father seems short next to him. He puts our shopping bags on top of the desk and sits in the chair next to him. I stand between my father's knees. In front of me, a poster hangs on the wall with calligraphic writing that says: "Credit is forbidden, and anger overridden."

Father says hello to Salim, who stands behind a sales

8

counter. He is wearing a *gallabiya* with a yellow overcoat that looks like the ones worn by janitors and office boys. He has a small woolen skullcap on his head, and his face is very pale. He answers my father in a voice that is cold and weak.

Abdel 'Alim says: "Young Abbas is all ready. Do you want to move the furniture tomorrow?"

My father nods his head to say yes: "It just better not be ruined by all the grease and butter."

"Not at all. I put all your things out of the way." He calls out: "Abbas! Where've you gone? You better not be dipping into that sauce of yours again."

A dark, barefoot man appears at the entrance to the shop. His eyes are bloodshot. He's wearing a dirty *gallabiya* and cap. He is moving slowly and he reeks.

"Move the rest of Khalil Bey's furniture from the warehouse tomorrow morning."

Abbas stammers: "I'm busy."

Abdel 'Alim says with more force: "It's a couch, two chairs and a table." He turns to father: "And I found a nice maid living nearby. She cleans and cooks and takes her salary by the month."

"How much?"

"Give her a pound."

Father asks him about the man that has moved into the vacant room next to ours. Abdel 'Alim plays with the tips of his moustache for a while, then says that he is a police constable.

"Is he married?"

"No."

Father asks Salim for ten eggs, fifty dirham worth of cheese, fifty dirham of halva, a box of Sheikh Al-Shareeb tea, a piece of Nablus soap, and a block of dark kitchen soap.

Salim asks rudely: "On your account?"

Father nods his head. Salim opens a large register and records our order in it, and father warns him: "Only fresh eggs, no rotten ones."

"Yes, of course, only fresh. We have butter from buffalo milk too."

Father shakes his head and asks for a pound of clarified butter instead. Salim asks in the same rude tone: "Do you have anything to put it in?"

"No."

His brother yells at him: "Just put it in a glass jar." He places our groceries in two paper bags, and my father gathers them up against his chest. We leave the shop. I ask him if I can carry one of the sacks. He tells me no because I'll drop it. *The reading textbook. Sirhan in the Field and at Home. He puts the eggs in his pockets and they are crushed. He tries to ride the lamb but it will not move. He drags the duck by a leash and chokes it to death.*

We head back to the alley. I ask him why he didn't buy butter. I like it with honey or molasses. I love the *murta*.

He tells me that Salim puts salt in the butter cones to cheat on the price, and that his brother Hajj Abdel 'Alim had warned him many times to stop doing it but it had not made any difference.

We go carefully into our darkened alley. We walk slowly. Weak light from the slats in the wooden shutters on the balconies. The blinds in the balcony of the house in front of ours are open, but the glass panels and the thin curtains behind them are closed. We stumble at the front of the house. We go up our couple of worn, broken-down steps. The darkened door to our apartment is to the right of the stairs that lead up to the higher floors. To the left, a black opening leads to the grocer's storehouse. I try not to look at it.

He hands me one of the bags and says: "Hold tight." He unbuttons his overcoat and pulls it to the side. Feels for the key in his coat pocket. He puts the key in the keyhole of the door and turns it. He pushes the door. I cling to his coat. We walk in cautiously.

He mutters a few times: "God protect us from Satan, the curséd. In the name of God, the Compassionate, the Merciful." He feels around with his hand until he finds the light switch. A weak ray of light comes from the dirty electric bulb that hangs from the middle of the ceiling. The light shines on a hall with a rectangular dining table. We stop in front of the door to the bedroom by the front door. Father takes another key out of his pocket. He leads me inside, and turns on the light.

He puts his bag on the desk, then turns his attention to my bag, gesturing to me as he takes it from me and puts it beside the other one. I sit on the edge of the large iron bed frame. To my right is the shuttered door to the small balcony. In front of me is the slanted wooden wardrobe. It rests on three wooden balls, each the size of a pomegranate, under its three corners. The fourth ball was lost during the move, so father put a small piece of wood under that corner. Still, the left flap would not close all the way, so it stays open a crack. A wooden clothes rack next to it, and the door is next to that. To the left, the desk is squeezed between the bed and the wall with the door.

He takes off his overcoat and hangs it on one of the rails of the clothes rack. Then he hangs his suit coat. On its button-hole, there is a round patch that is bronze-colored and has the words "Quit Egypt!" written on it. He puts his fez over the top of the clothes rack, showing the balding top of his head surrounded by hair that is almost all white. He puts on a skull-cap made of goat's wool, camel colored, with a wide border turned up to its tip. He keeps on the grey woolen waistcoat with wooden buttons. He puts on his brown robe and ties it up with a thin red rope belt. He wraps a wide scarf, made from the same material as the skullcap, around his neck and chest.

I untie my shoes and set them down next to the door. I put on my slippers without taking off my socks. I take off my coat and throw it over the back of the office chair. I do the same with my sweater and my shirt, then I shudder from the cold. After I put on my pyjamas, I put the sweater back on. He grabs a canvas bag nearby on the desk and takes out a loaf of twice-baked bread. A small black cockroach hops out of the bag. I stumble back, away from the desk. He asks me if I would rather have cheese or halva. My eye is stuck on the spot where the cockroach crawled out. I say I'm not hungry. He says: "Shall I make you an egg with dates?" I shake my head. He puts the loaf back in the bag.

I start to get my school bag ready. I make sure I have my blotting paper and ink bottle. I notice he is still wearing his trousers and shoes. I ask him: "Why don't you undress?"

He says: "I want to sauté the meat first."

"Leave it till morning."

"Then it'll spoil."

He bends over and pulls back the bed sheet used as a dust cover. Shoes, plates, cartons, and metal pots. Syringe for an enema. He grabs a metal pan. He looks around for its lid until finally he finds it. Then he leaves the room and I follow him. He takes hold of the package of meat and empties it into the pan. He heads towards the start of the dark hallway in front of our room. The toilet with its door hanging open and a sickening smell coming out. A large bathroom is closed, its door held shut by a wooden latch. A metal sink has a faucet mounted on the wall above it. He washes off the meat well. He walks to the kitchen at the end of the hall. He enters with me hanging on his clothes from behind. He picks up a box of matches and lights one of them. The light falls on the side of the wall covered in water. There is a wooden table with a kerosene primus lamp on it. He squashes a big red cockroach with his foot. He presses on the primus lamp several times, then lights a match and moves it close to the opening that lets the fumes out. The flame flickers. I grab on to him and blink. *The beauty dangles the long braids of her hair from the window so that Hassan the Brave can climb them. Suddenly, the ghoul can be seen coming from far away. It is a big blur that looks like a huge bale of hair riding the wind as it covers wide spaces, kicking up dust and gravel around it. It stops under the window and cries up to the woman: "Unfasten yourself and let down your long braids; take in the ghoul from the heat, give him shade."*

The stove crackles. The colors of its flame spread out. He turns the meat over with his spoon. He lifts up the pan and pours out its juice into the sink.

I ask: "Isn't it done yet?"

He says the meat has to come to a hard boil to get rid of all the microbes. He opens a jar of liquid butter, digs out two spoonfuls, and throws them in the pan. He flips the meat a few times, then adds the water. He throws in a pinch of salt, then another of black pepper, then covers it.

He goes with me to the small bathroom to pee. When I complain about the smell, he says the plunger is broken. I recite the Quranic "verse of the throne" the way he taught me. He gives me a gentle shove to help me up on to the base of the stone toilet. I resist and he climbs up with me to stand by my side. He holds me by my shoulders while I undo the buttons on my underpants. I look up at the wall. Rays of weak hall lighting beam down on the big black spots. Suddenly a black spot comes flying up. I cling to my father's clothes, but he tells me: "Don't worry. It's just a house spider."

We go back to the kitchen. He flips the meat and adds more water. He waits until the water boils, and then he turns off the flame. He carries the pan to the hall while I hang on to him. He leaves it on top of the sideboard. We go back to the hallway and he washes his hands with soap.

We go into our room and he closes the door carefully. The door to the balcony shakes violently and father says that it is the winds of the month of *Amsheer* with its dust devils and whirlwinds. He grabs an old *gallabiya* from one of the hangers and uses it to plug the open crack between the door and the bare tiled floor. He puts another piece of cloth under the door of the balcony. He places his head on the floor and studies the empty space between the wardrobe and the wall, then bends down again and stares at the long narrow open space between the base of the wardrobe and the floor tiles. He pulls open the two doors of the wardrobe and takes a look inside. Lifts up the end of the bed sheet. By now, he is panting from the effort. He takes off his robe and hangs it on a knob of the rack. He recites: "There is only one God, none but Him, the Living, the Eternal, Who takes not slumber, nor rest."

I climb up into the high metal bed before him. He follows me. I slide over to my place next to the wall. He bends over and wraps the covers around me while he keeps reciting. He finishes up the verse of the throne, then follows it up with another. His voice becomes softer and softer until the words become faint. He brushes my face with his warm hand. My eyelids fall in surrender. *The ghoul smells the scent of Hassan the Brave, then says: "Fee, fi, fo, fum; I smell the putrid scent of a human."*

He raises his hand and I open my eyes. He puts his hand back. I close my eyes. He lifts his hand again and I open my eyes again. *Hassan the Brave and the beauty jump at the chance to escape when the ghoul goes out. The beauty paints everything in the castle with henna and forgets about the drums. The ghoul comes back and calls out to the girl, then the objects painted in henna start to spin around her. The sieve calls out in a beautiful singsong voice in harmony with its movements: "Straaaain, straaaain, straaaain." The quern says: "Griiiind, griiind, griiiind." The cutting board sings: "Choppp, choppp, choppppp." But the forgotten drum takes revenge for itself by crying: "Hassan the Brave, took her and flew away!"*

I follow his movements. He stands up straight. He bends over. He rubs his knees. He pulls off the wool wrap, the robe, and the vest. He slips his braces off his shoulders. He sits on the edge of the bed. He pulls off his socks and shoes, then puts on long woolen stockings. He lifts his right leg and pulls on his trousers, then slips on the other leg. He gets back up. He pulls off his tie and his shirt. All that's left is the woolen undershirt with its long sleeves and the woolen long johns. He presses his feet into his clogs. Puts his clothes on the hanger. He bends over and spreads his legs out. He has a hard time untying the laces of the hernia belt between his thighs. He strains to get out of it and throws it on the desk then gasps with relief. He rubs his knees and then lets loose a loud fart.

He puts on a striped flannel *gallabiya*. Tosses the shawl over his shoulders and chest. He stretches his hand to his mouth and pulls out his teeth, then he puts them in a cup of water on the desk. He drinks out of a jug in a metal pan on the ground. Wipes his mouth and his moustache with the back of his hand. He fills a cup with rusty nails up with water, so he can have a drink as soon as he gets up. He raises his hands to his head and presses on the skullcap. Takes two steps. He stretches his hand out toward the dresser. He puts out the light. Climbs up next to me. He tucks himself under the sheets and blankets, and rolls over to me to make sure that I'm also covered. His hand stays there on top of me. *My mother's round face draws near. She rocks me while she sings the song coming out of the radio: "Sleep o love of my soooul."*

I n the beauty of the spring, your birthday draws near,
  You are more splendid than spring, and more dear."

We repeat the chorus behind the music teacher. A big colored handkerchief dangles out of the breast pocket of his suit jacket. He will be coming with us to Abideen Palace for the king's birthday. They give us sandwiches made from yellow cheddar cheese. We also get a piece of halva made from crushed sesame. Monday will be a half day. The English teacher writes the date at the top of the blackboard. I can see clearly what's written, thanks to my glasses. A rumbling starts up in the back rows of the class. The teacher turns around and goes to his chair. His clothes look all fancy and expensive. The cuffs of his trouser legs are wide, in the style of the day. They are stiff over the fronts of his shoes and cover his heels at the back, down to the point where they touch the floor. He says without looking up at any of us: "Whoever doesn't want to have a lesson, please help himself to the exit."

The older students in the back rows get up and leave the room. I take my six-shooter out of my drawer and I follow them. The outer hallway runs down to the empty courtyard. A total calm has settled over the school. The way is empty. I bend over so I can pass underneath the windows of the ongoing classes. Another classroom. The teacher's lounge. Its door is closed. I put my eye against the keyhole. There's a rectangular table with a bare-headed man sitting at the end. He's bald. His fez is in front of him on top of several notebooks. I manage to recognize that he is the science teacher. He looks strange with no fez and no hair. He picks up one of the notebooks. He's staring disapprovingly at the corner of the table. I can see a number of hands playing cards at the edge of my vision.

I catch up with some students on the stairs. We sneak out to a courtyard at the back where an annex to the school is being built. They all spread out behind the piles of sand and gravel. They take out their handkerchiefs, fold them once, spread them over their noses, then tie them at the back of their heads. I take off my glasses, which have given me the nickname "Gandhi," then I tie my own handkerchief over my nose before I put them back on. I squat down behind a pile of gravel, holding on to my six-shooter. *The courtyard of the old school is surrounded by tall black fencing so we can't see out. I buy a yam with hot pepper from a small opening in its side. We find an old staircase with worn out steps leading down. A student says that the schoolhouse used to be the palace of an emir. He's sure that there's a magic well underneath it. We are scared but go down anyway. We stumble upon a lizard. My mother tells me it's a princess in disguise.*

I stay in my place behind the pile of gravel without anyone calling for me. The bell rings. We go back up to our Arabic grammar class with heavy steps. The teacher has a skinny build. He has a long neck with a thick *kaffiyeh* wrapped around it. His shoulders are constantly wiggling inside his suit coat. We all know that he just stopped wearing his *jubbah* and turban less than a year ago.

I change places with Fathi so I can sit next to Maher. He has a ring full of keys, a Biro ballpoint pen, a Waterman fountain pen, and a soft, fat eraser. He puts them in a row in front of him on the surface of his writing desk. The teacher explains to us, without standing up, the rules of the stem form of the verb, the derivative stem forms, and the phonetic verbs. He doesn't bother to stand in front of the board because he is so short. He asks one of the taller students to write on it: "The prince of poets addresses the young men." We open up the book, *Selections of the Masters*. We read, along with him, a poem by Ahmad Showqi. He scolds us for our ignorance. In my notebook I write down what the words mean. I spell a word wrongly. I try to rub it out with my dried up, cheap eraser. I borrow Maher's soft one.

The bell rings. I lift the tabletop of my desk. I take out the textbooks and notepads that I need for tomorrow's homework. I put them in my satchel. I let down the desktop, take out my key, and lock it.

No sooner have I walked out into the open-air hallway than a cold wind slaps against me. I bury my neck under my *kaffiyeh*, and I shrink inside my clothes. It's hard to drag my feet along. I move along the pavement outside the school, and I put off crossing the main street until I get to the square. I notice a little rectangle of iron. I want to kick it along my way, but then I remember my father's warnings about bombs that explode at no more than a touch and that look like a medicine bottle, a fountain pen, or a toy. I look at it carefully then move away from it.

A pavement of multicolored gravel. A fenced-in villa with steel grating. I steal a look from between the poles. A wooden table and two chairs are at the side of the garden. The door to the villa is shut. I start walking again. The Jewish school. It's made from pink bricks. There's no outer wall surrounding it, like at our school. A flier calls for aid for Palestinian refugees. A black banner reads: "No negotiations without complete British withdrawal!" Another says: "Hey diddle diddle!" The school's windows are at street level. Long halls with rows of dining tables behind them. The students eat and make noise. I keep walking to the corner, then I turn left. I pass next to the wall of the school. The road gets a little bit steep and it has more trees. The red and yellow flowers that started to bloom at the beginning of the summer have dried and fallen over the pavement now that it's autumn. *We try to hunt the sparrows with our bows and arrows, but we don't get a single one.*

I find myself in front of our old home. It's also of pale yellow brick. The iron door is the first thing you see. Around the door is an old crumbling house. In front of it, there's a big crater made by a bomb dropped by German planes. I put my satchel on the ground and lean against the wall of the school.

The house sits at the fork between two streets divided by a nasty open space surrounded by fencing made of metal poles. It used to be a storage house for the tram. The metal poles of the fencing are secured at the bottom by railings barely raised a foot off the ground. *We stand on the railings between the poles and puff up our cheeks, then we toot our horns and drive.*

20

The first street heads towards a shanty town and the second towards a factory that makes fezzes next to a square where the fair to celebrate the prophet's birthday takes place. At the point of coming together, there's a row of carriages with the heads of their attached horses buried in sacks of straw. The two streets come together where there's a little bit of a downhill slope in the road, beginning past our house and going down to the street that leads to the square. At the corner, there's a nursery with flowers for sale.

The place where we live takes up the first floor and has two windows looking down on to the street. The curtains cover one of them, but in the other, only the glass is closed. It reflects the trees and the blue sky. *With my finger I trace my name and the names of my father and mother in the condensation that's covered the closed window. I think to myself about the workers rushing to the factory, each one carrying a snack in his handkerchief. There are small children among them. The morning whistle of the factory blows, then I leave our house. I am met by the smell of exhaust from burners. I lift my head towards the window and see my father in his round white skullcap following me with his eyes from behind the glass. I cross the road to the pavement in front of the Jewish school. I pass by an old man with a big red turban, leaning on a walking stick with one of his hands while resting his back against the school wall. I give him two millimes as my father has taught me. I turn to see him in the window one last time. I adjust the book pack on my back and push my cold hands far down into the pockets of my jacket. I wind my way through the crush of students from the Jewish school. Boys and girls dressed in blue. I bounce towards the main street that goes to my school. The fog that I love so much swallows me.*

I carry my satchel and I turn to follow the road. I move into a small passage. A shop to help find a maid. A wooden partition has little openings between the panels. Behind them there's a bench with girls sitting on it. One of them wears a black headcloth and a *gallabiya*. Next to her a girl is dressed like the *fellah* women. I come out to Farouk street. I wait for the signal from the traffic policeman. I walk in front of the Abdelmalik bakery and the Alsabeel pharmacy. I read its sign: "The acting manager is Helmy Rafael." A few steps farther and I have entered Al-Nuzha Street that leads to our new house.

Father puts on his robe. He opens the glass door to the balcony. He pushes the wooden shutter to the outside. He fastens it to the metal loop in the wall with its hook. The pale light of the morning sneaks into the room. He closes the glass pane and studies the balcony across the way.

I cough and complain to him that my throat is sore. He touches my forehead. He probes underneath my ear, feeling for my tonsils. Then he leaves the room and throws himself into making a plate of fava bean paste with hot oil.

He puts the plate on to the wooden four-sided table that Abbas has brought out from storage. The table's at the same level with the bed and spread almost all the way across it are the plate of beans, the piece of white cheese wrapped in paper, the loaf of bread, and the split key lime. He takes a small onion from under the bed and puts it down between the door and the wall without bothering to peel it. He pulls the door into the room then pushes with it against the onion a little bit. He puts the door back where it was and catches the onion before it falls down. He takes out its heart, which has started to stick out, and he throws the outer skin to the side. He says it's the best way not to lose its taste and to stay healthy.

He sits down cross-legged on the bed. I drag over the desk chair and sit in front of him. He squeezes lime juice over the beans. I dip in a small piece of the bread. I chew an end of it without really caring. I say that I don't like fava beans. He says that when he was a schoolboy, he would grab his breakfast from a pot of cold leftovers from the night before. His mother would call down to him from the upper floor each morning: "There's a pot of leftovers in the skylight."

We finish breakfast. We go out of the room and rinse the dishes at the wash basin. The doorbell rings. He opens the door for the milkman. He brings a small pan and takes a gallon. He lights the fire and puts the pan over it until the milk boils, then puts a metal pitcher in its place to make the cinnamon. He keeps standing next to it until the cinnamon water has come to the boil several times. He pours me a cup then adds the milk to it. I bring the cup to my mouth. I notice a smell of gas. I give the cup back to him. He gets mad and sits drinking from his cup quietly.

The doorbell rings again. I rush to the door and open it. Um Nazira comes in. Short and skinny. Her hair is wrapped in a black scarf tied over her forehead with white hairs hanging from the sides. Her face is pale and her eyes are sunken. She takes off her black sandals and leaves them by the door. She puts a bag of vegetables on the dining table. She says she was late because the women who volunteer with the cholera service stopped her on her way and took her to the inoculation center.

Father gives her the leftovers from our breakfast. When

she sits down on the floor, he tells her she can sit on one of the dining-room chairs. He asks about her husband and children. He pays her for the vegetables she brought. He makes himself a cup of Turkish coffee over a Sterno can in the small brass coffee pot. He pours it into a hand-painted china cup and carries it by its saucer. I follow him to our room and he sits cross-legged on the bed. He sips at the coffee slowly. I put the chair back in its place at the desk. I sit and take out my math notebook.

I start to solve my homework questions. I get stuck on one of the problems. I look up at him. He can add, subtract, multiply and divide without even using a pen and pad, but the scowl on his face scares me from asking for help. He lights his black cigarette. I try to think of a trick. I remember the vocabulary lesson from Arabic class. I ask him what type of house we have. I list off on my fingers the types I have learned: a palace, a castle, a hermitage, a cellar, a shack. He shakes his head and says our house is in its own class. I show him my math problem and he solves it for me.

I put on my glasses and walk out of our room and into the living area. Um Nazira lines up the dishes she has just washed on the marble surface of the sideboard. I pause in front of the door of the constable's room. I steal a glance through the keyhole but I can't see anything but the edge of a bed with its covers all ruffled in a stack. I put my ear to the hole, but I can't hear any movement.

I go back behind the dining table. I move away from the glass door that leads to the skylight where the cold wind is leaking inside. I turn around again and stop in front of the door of the third room. I turn the doorknob and go in. It has a worn and ragged wooden floor full of holes. Our old furniture: a rocking chair made of wicker with one side torn off, two armchairs and a couch. One of the armchairs has a sunken seat.

The room is cold. The paint on the walls is cracked, showing the plaster underneath it. Some of the cracks are covered with colored paper. I walk up to them. They're pages from a green photography magazine fastened with staples. A picture of King Farouk when he was young and pretty, with short trousers and a fez. Another picture shows him in a convertible with his three beautiful sisters. Another shows him next to his father, King Fuad, with his pointy moustache and its long handlebars curving upwards. I reach with my hand to touch the shiny surface of the pictures. The dry plaster behind it falls off. Um Nazira calls me to come out so she can sweep the room.

Father sits on the bed with his prayer beads in his hand. The blinds of the balcony across from us are open, but the lace curtains hang down behind the glass door. It's small and narrow like our own balcony and the ones on the first floor. Above it are two big balconies next to each other in the same apartment. A clerk lives there who is married to two wives, each with her own balcony. One of them is open, its covers spread out over the ledge to take the sun. The other is closed up. That means he spent the night there. Today, it will be the other balcony's turn.

I stand behind the glass. I press my cheek against the pane so I can see the house on the corner. Sabry Effendi's window is open. His wife appears for an instant then disappears. Short and fat. Her face is covered with pock marks from heat rash.

Also her children: Siham, the oldest girl, Soha, the middle girl, then Selma, the youngest girl, and Samir, the youngest of them all.

Um Nazira calls us and tells us to leave the room so she can sweep and mop it. Father rocks himself off the bed. He puts his feet into his clogs. She opens the door to the balcony, drags the rug out, and spreads it over the ledge. She sweeps the floor. We watch her from the doorway between the room and the hall. He's scared that she'll try to get in the pockets of his clothes hanging on the rack.

She finishes sweeping and puts her swath of sackcloth into the mop bucket, then she takes it out and flings the water around over the surface of the floor. She bends over at the waist to wipe the floor with it. Her *gallabiya* comes up over her bony knee caps. She wrings out the cloth in the bucket. She dries the floor, then straightens up, panting.

She picks up the bucket and gets ready to leave the room. Father stops her. He points to a wet patch near the balcony. She says she didn't see it, but anyway it'll be dry in no time if we leave the balcony door open. He screams at her: "Do what I tell you!" She obeys but doesn't really want to.

My father steps into the room and closes the door to the balcony. He stays there for a moment, keeping his eyes on the balcony facing ours.

Um Nazira calls out from the living area: "The water is hot." I pick up my clean clothes and my loofah and leave our room. Father follows me carrying an old newspaper. He closes the door, locks it, and puts the key in the pocket of his robe. We head towards the guest room. The iron washbasin is in the middle. There's a primus stove with a water tap over it that gives off wafts of steam. A large can of cold water. Father takes off his robe. He squats. He mixes the cold water with the hot and then tests its temperature with his hand. I try to remember what the science teacher taught us about how to measure the boiling point. *The water boils over the primus stove. Mother fills a metal pitcher with boiling water. She adds water from the tap, then she pours it over my naked body. She fills the pitcher with the hot water again, but this time, she forgets to add the cool tap water before she pours it over me. I scream. My father rushes to me. He carries me to the bedroom. He dries me off tenderly. He sprinkles white powder on me. He dresses me and takes me with him to the mosque.*

I take my clothes off and plunge into the water in the basin. He scrubs my head with the Nablus soap and my body with the loofah. He asks me to stand up, so he can rinse me off with clean water. He dries me off. I look up at the picture of the king on the wall. He wraps the newspaper around my chest and I put my clothes on over it. He calls Um Nazira to throw out the dirty water and refill the can.

We go back to our room. He takes off the robe and *gallabiya*. He turns away from me and takes off his woolen shirt, showing me his bare back. He asks me to scratch it. I put on my glasses. I scratch around the three blue pimples spread across his back. His body is white, just like his face and his arms up to the elbows. He tells me to look for the lice hidden in the seams of his shirt. He points me to the crevices in the seams on each side and asks me to look closely at them. I find one fat white louse. There's a black spot on its back. I like that kind better than the thin black ones. I put it on my left thumbnail and I press against it with my right thumbnail. I listen to its splat. He hangs up the shirt, saying: "That's enough."

He picks out clean clothes from the dresser. He says in a hushed tone: "Watch out for Um Nazira." I follow him to the door of our room. Um Nazira sits at the table in the living area whittling the skin off bulbs of taro.

I sit at my desk. I get up. I steal a glance at Um Nazira from the crack in the door. She slices her knife through one of the bulbs and begins to cut it into small cubes.

My father comes out of the guest room wearing a clean *gallabiya*. He tells Um Nazira to throw out the dirty water and dry off the floor of the room.

She says: "After I'm done with this."

He says the floor has to be dried right away before water gathers in the crevices of the hard wood flooring. She's mad as she gets up and goes past him to the kitchen. She takes up her mop rag and bucket and goes into the guest room. She comes out after a little bit with the bucket and goes to the kitchen, then she comes back in and sits down. He tells her to go back and wash her hands. She goes to wash them. I tell him in a hushed voice that she didn't wash the taro after peeling it. She comes back and sits down and starts cutting again. He asks her if she washed it after peeling it. She says she'll do it after she finishes cutting it. He yells at her, saying: "Didn't I tell you to wash it first and then dry it with a towel?"

She says: "It doesn't matter."

He says: "Do what I say."

Her lips tighten and she goes on cutting the bulbs without saying anything.

He takes a razor out of his shaving kit. A little box to hold cigarettes made of cardboard. He unfastens the case for the razor that has a picture of a crocodile on it. He puts his right foot over the edge of the bed. He bends forward and slices off the corn on his little toe. He says it's from the pointy toed shoes that he wore as a young man, after the style of the day. He cuts a corn off his left foot and puts the blade back into its case. He takes out little scissors. He cuts at his hardened toenails with some effort. Leaves the room to wash his hands. He comes back. He puts on socks made of wool.

The sound of the Friday sermon comes out of Um Zakia's radio. She lives on the first floor of the house next door and her window looks down over the skylight. Father gets up off the bed and stands straight up. He walks over to the wall. He places his palms on it then brings them to his face and wipes it with them both while he mutters little prayers begging for God's help. He finishes with the ritual and starts to get ready for prayer. *I stop my red car at the door of the dining room with my hands on the steering wheel, waiting all in a hurry with my eyes focused on his frowning face. I pretend I'm like the drivers waiting at the traffic light. The imam finishes the Friday sermon and starts to ask blessings on the king. My father unfolds his rug in the guest room. I am bored as I wait and so I start to count how many times he bows. He turns his head to the right to ask peace on the guardian angel on the right shoulder, then he does the same to the guardian angel on the left shoulder. Before he gets up and folds his rug, I've shot off.*

He prays on the bed. I go out to the living area. I take a plate down from the sideboard. I pour some molasses on to it, and study it closely to make sure there are no ants in it. I add some tahini from a jar. I get a loaf of bread and have to work hard to balance everything. The plate wobbles and a few drops fall to the floor. I put the plate down on the table. I lick a drop of molasses from my finger. Um Nazira spots the drops of molasses on the floor and says angrily: "I'm not going to mop again."

The prayer ends and father appears in the doorway. He asks her what she's screaming about. He is mad as he tells her that he will not let her raise her voice to me. He orders her to wipe up the bits of molasses. She gives in gloomily. He waits until she's finished and gets up to go back to the table, then he tells her to wash her hands with soap.

We go back to our room. I am waiting for him to scold me, but he doesn't. I take my place behind my desk and open the math notebook. He tells me to keep an eye on Um Nazira to make sure she doesn't drink all our ghee. He sits cross legged on top of the bed. He takes hold of a long string of dark wooden prayer beads. He starts to count on it, muttering to himself in the name of "the Gentle."

I steal a glance at Um Nazira through the crack in the door. I see her carrying the pan of taro, headed toward the kitchen. I follow her. I glance sideways at the bathroom. I come closer to the kitchen door softly. I stop and cling to the wall. I pull my head back a little for fear that she might see me.

She puts the pan on the stove and adds water to it. She peels the garlic and chops it into small pieces with her knife. She throws it in with the chard in a metal skillet with a long handle. She grabs the jar of ghee and takes a spoonful. She throws it into the skillet with the garlic. I hold my breath when she sticks the spoon back into the jar. She fills it again. Is she going to eat it herself? I watch her hand as it moves toward the skillet.

I feel movement behind me. Father is coming up sneakily. He puts his hand on my shoulder. He cranes his neck to try to see her. She grabs the pot of taro with a towel and picks it up off the fire. She puts it on the table. She puts the skillet over the flame then stirs the mixture with a spoon. She leans forward to take a good look at it then heads towards the jar of ghee with the spoon in her hand. Father tilts his head some more to see what she is doing. She turns suddenly and catches sight of him. She screams. Her hand slips off the handle of the pan and what's in it spills all over the floor. She beats her chest with her hand: "You scared me. Damn you!"

Father goes into the kitchen and yells: "Damn you and damn your life! Can't you be careful?"

She screams back: "What kind of a job is this?"

"Pick up what you've spilled."

She pushes him and goes toward the front door: "Just see for yourself who'll pick up for you. I'm leaving."

Father screams after her: "Then go to hell."

We walk behind a woman wrapped up in a wide black sheet. Her face is covered with a burka that shows only her eyes and that is held up by a shiny brass chain that comes to a point over her nose with a light fabric hanging down like a flap covering her mouth. She is walking with quick steps while she clutches the sheet around her body. From the corner of my eye, I pick up father's glances at the swaying of her full bottom. I trip over a brick and he scolds me: "Be careful."

Narrow crowded alleyways. Old doors and stone benches in front of tiny shops. Smells of mud, decay, and axle grease. She stops until a vegetable cart passes, pulled along by a horse. She stretches the black sheet around her body, making its shape more clear. A beautiful perfume comes from her body. *I go out to the living room. I look around for my mother. The annoying sound of the stove's fire comes from the kitchen. I steal inside their bedroom. The bed. Across their mattress is a lace bedspread. I take the blue perfume bottle from on top of the dresser and I smell its rim.*

She moves away from us, then disappears. A darkened alley. Narrow stairs with worn-out steps. Father lights a match. We go up a few floors. We stop in front of a door with two glass windows. One of them is covered over with sackcloth. He knocks on the door and an angry-sounding voice inside calls out: "Who's there?" He knocks again. An old woman opens up, carrying an oil lamp. She lifts the lamp up high to see us. The light falls down over a face that is pale and frowning. A droopy eye tries to stare out from its hiding place under a swollen eyelid. "Is Sheikh Affifi here?"

She stands back for us without saying anything. Old furniture in piles. A door is opened by a skinny old man wrapped in a caftan made of shiny, striped cloth. He greets father and leads him over to a table with an oil lamp on top of it. He makes a big effort just to walk and teeters from side to side, on the verge of falling. He clutches the caftan to his body as he sits in a chair by the table. Father sits in front of him and I stand next to father. He takes two glasses and pours some liquid into them. One of them smells like musk. He takes a reed pen and dips it into one. He pulls over a plate made of white china. He puts his eyes right next to it. It's decorated with boxes and dark lettering. The light from the lamp spreads across his thin, clean-shaven face and his two eyes that never stop blinking. Father's eyes stay fixed on the pen. Framed Quranic verses are hung on the wall. There's a Coca-Cola sign too that says it quenches thirst in the winter also. The chairs are covered with dirty cloth. One of them has a sunken chair that almost touches the ground.

I move away from father. I come closer to the door that's left ajar. I turn my eyes to the open crack. Right in front of me, there's a blue circle with a surface that stands out. The bad eye of the old woman who opened the door for us becomes clear in it. She is craning her body, bending her knees, trying to hear. I step back and begin to feel for the safety of father, clinging to him. His head is tilted and he's taking in the words of the old man. His bottom lip is plump and dangling. He tells father: "How do you feel about reading my horoscope for me?"

Father says in a surprised voice: "Who, me?"

"Yes, you. I'll teach you. It's very simple."

"Well then do it yourself."

"I wish. It doesn't work that way."

"Well, what do you want to know?"

"How much longer shall I live?"

Father sighs and says: You've already lived long, and you'll only live a little longer."

He gives him a silver coin. He asks him about a good woman who can clean and cook. He says he's ready to marry her if she comes from good stock.

We leave the house and go to board the tram. I ask him how long he will live. He says he'll live to 100. We pass in front of the chemist. It is closed even though it's not closing time. Father heads towards a hand cart with a pile of date paste on it, covered in a sheer white cloth. A light shines down from a mantle lamp fastened over the middle of it. He buys a pound. Hajj Abdel 'Alim, the neighborhood sheikh, starts to call out to us. We go into his shop. Hajj is behind his desk. Next to him is another sheikh, Sheikh Fadhl. Wearing a turban, and he has no teeth. He is holding the newspaper *Akhbar al Youm* in his hand. My father tells Selim that one of the eggs he sold him two days ago was rotten. He sits down on a chair and I sit on the one next to him. Abdel 'Alim says while he's clearing his throat that the chemist's owner sold a copybook at a price that was two millimes over the regulation price, and that he was sentenced to six months and a fine of 100 pounds.

Father asks him about Maged Effendi. The neighborhood sheik says: "He's gone to Zarakish."

"Who's Zarakish?"

"You mean you don't know? It's the genie he's married."

"He married a genie? How do you mean?"

Abdel 'Alim says that a white cat fastened itself to him and started to share his bed. Then one day it stood on its two hind legs, and stretched upwards. Then it peeled off its fur and a beautiful woman appeared. He asked her name and she said: "Zarakish." She began to dance and then asked him to marry her, saying that she was Muslim like him.

Father asks about the butcher that disappeared. Abdel 'Alim says that he married a second wife without telling the first. Father asks: "A spring chicken?" No, he answers. She's a divorcée who has been married three times before. He left the shop to his son and left the neighborhood altogether. He says that Um Nazira came to him today and begged him for sympathy. She's ready to kiss his foot if he'll let her come back. Father says sternly: "No. I don't want her." Abdel 'Alim asks him: "Have you tried the Maid Services Office?" Father says he doesn't trust the girls that they send, and besides that, the agent takes a big commission.

A fancy looking brown-skinned man comes in wearing a white shirt with a starched collar and a fez tilted slightly to the left. The neighborhood sheikh greets him: "Welcome, Refaat Effendi." Father lifts me on to his lap to give Refaat my seat. He sits down and says that today he defended a woman facing the death penalty. She is twenty-three years old and married to an old man who is older than sixty. They sent him to the hospital throwing up violently.

Abdel 'Alim asks: "Cholera?"

The lawyer shakes his head: "Cholera's on holiday until the summer."

'Then what the hell?"

The lawyer says that the old man accused the wife of trying to poison him so she could get rid of him and marry a young buck her own age. The physician of the court testified that the old man had drunk an amount of whisky mixed with camphor oil.

He is quiet for a while, then says: "All the evidence was against the girl. She would've been thrown to the lions if I hadn't asked the old codger three questions."

Everyone except father asks him in one voice: "What were they?"

He says: "I asked him if he was in the habit of rubbing his legs with camphor oil before he went to bed. The man said yes. I asked him where he kept the bottle of camphor oil. He said on the night stand next to the bed. Then I asked him: "And where exactly was the whisky?" He said it was by the camphor oil."

He looks around at us full of pride: "The court drew the conclusion that the man got drunk, reached for the whisky bottle, grabbed the camphor oil instead, and took a sip."

The sheikh wearing the turban looks at father and says: "That's what he gets for marrying a woman that's his daughter's age." Father's face twists into a frown. Then the neighborhood sheikh steps in and asks if father wants to go in with the rest of the group in buying *Al Ahram* newspaper. Every-one would pitch in a piastre and they could get the paper for the whole month. Father says that he reads the paper at the shoeshine shop, "and anyway, today's news is the same as yesterday's."

Refaat Effendi says: "You can say that again. Look at the story today about the Yemeni Jews and how the English are smuggling them into Palestine. Ever since the partition, ships keep coming and going, gathering them up from near and far."

Then he lowers his voice and adds that the university students tore up the king's picture and made fun of his fooling around. They chanted that he was "Ruler of Egypt, Sudan … and the dancer Samia Gamal!" Sheikh Fadhl says that the king dumped Samia Gamal long ago and replaced her with Um Kalthoum. The lawyer says that an electric air-conditioner was installed in her private villa. The turbaned sheikh says his son got a university degree by being granted a tuition waiver, then he went to work in the Qena district office for six pounds a month at the ninth clerical rank. The lawyer says that Lutfi Al-Sayyid Pasha, as president of the Academy of the Arabic Language, makes nine pounds a month, with a stipend for in-flation of three pounds. He was getting four pounds a month when he was appointed at the council fifty years ago. The sheikh says: "An *oka* of sugar with a ration certificate is 75 mil-limes and it costs 200 on the black market."

Hajj Abdel 'Alim asks: "Did you read Fikry Abaza? He's de-manding a tax increase on the rich, limits on the monarchy, redistribution of land, and a war on inflation."

Sheikh Fadhl comments: "Calling for limits on land ownership is sacrilegious. Verily, the Sheikh of Al Azhar himself issued a fatwa saying so." The neighborhood sheikh cuts him off: "Let's get off politics, please. Have you heard the latest joke? It goes that the Heliopolis tram has two lines. One stops at Manshiyat al Bakry terminal and the other at Manshiyat al Boozem terminal. One day a girl with huge breasts gets on and asks the ticket collector if it stops at Manshiyat al Bakry. He stares at her breasts and says: 'No, we go to Manshiyat al Boozem and we stop there.'"

Everyone laughs except for father. He pushes to his feet and excuses himself, then walks out. I ask him when we get to our quarter what the joke meant and why everyone laughed. He doesn't answer. I ask him: "What does the neighborhood sheikh do?"

"He sits for an hour every day at the police station notarizing witness statements and personal papers for the people of the quarter."

"What's his salary for doing that?"

"He doesn't get a salary. He takes tips from the people. It comes to a tidy sum."

I ask as we go into our house: "How old is mama?"

He answers me sharply: "Twenty-six."

We get off tram number three at its last stop at Abbas-siya Square. We take the white tram that goes toward Heliopolis. We head out alongside the English army barracks. Trees line the way on either side. Daylight is about to disappear. A military hospital: wooden balconies along a two-story building.

We exit the tram at the last station in Al-Ismailiya Square. A coffeehouse surrounded by glass. An old Armenian man pushes around a cart with a pianola. A skating rink. The dark street is lined by houses with walled-in gardens. The scent of jasmine. A closed metal door has a chain and padlock hanging down. We go in from a side door. A passage paved with colored tiles. We walk up wide marble steps. The door at the top of the stairs is closed. It is only used in the summer. We knock on the door next to it. Saadiya, the wife of the doorman, opens. Her body is thin and her face pale. We are greeted by Uncle Fahmi, my sister's husband: "Welcome! Welcome! You're brightening up the place." He is tall and broad and wears a thick, checkered woolen robe. His cigarette is in his hand. He works as an accountant in a foreign company. He is full of energy as he leads us to the terrace room on the east side. It has a wooden floor. Father takes off his overcoat. Uncle Fahmi takes it from him. We sit down on a couch facing the door. There is a metal table in front of us with a closed backgammon set on top of it.

Nabila comes to join us. She's my half-sister. Her body is thin like mine with long smooth hair. She wears a flannel robe and a pair of pink house slippers with embroidered cloth flowers on their tops. Thick white socks show inside them. She is holding a pair of fingernail clippers. She kisses father on the cheek and he answers with a noisy kiss. She screams with laughter: "Your moustache is prickly." She sits next to him on the other side and continues clipping her nails. She is short-sighted and has to bend her head over.

Father asks after Showqi and Shareen. My sister says that they are at Samira's. Her husband sits in the chair in front of us. He lifts the cover of the backgammon set. My sister says to him: "Let him catch his breath first." He smiles carefully and looks at father with narrowed eyes. He passes his hand over his short moustache, then takes out a metal cigarette case from the pocket of his robe. It's the Three Fives brand. He opens it and takes out a cigarette. He lights it with a flat lighter. His fingers are thick with round and carefully trimmed nails and yellow, nicotine-stained tips.

Father asks: "Is that a new lighter?"

"A Ronson. Press it once and it lights, then goes out by itself."

He reaches his right arm across the side of the chair carefully and flicks his cigarette ash. My sister notices what he does and says sharply: "Where's the ashtray?" He gets up in a rush without losing his fixed smile: "Yes, madam. As you say, madam." He grabs an ashtray from on top of a small table with thin gilded legs. He sets it next to the backgammon set. He looks at himself in a round mirror on the opposite wall. He straightens the patch of hair on his head with his left hand. My sister puts down her nail clippers and takes up a comb, then drags it through her long smooth hair.

Uncle Fahmi takes a careful sideways look at my sister: "White or black, Khalil Bey?" Father adjusts himself in his seat, lights his black cigarette, takes a puff on it, and sets it down on the edge of the ashtray. He throws the dice. He leans forward to see what he has. He keeps me back with his arm as he says: "Black, just like my luck."

Saadiya brings a tray of green tea. Uncle Fahmi offers us a square box made of tin. I take a piece of chocolate out of it that is about the size of a key lime. I unwrap its silver foil. I unfold the paper strip inside that tells your fortune and read: "O you night owl." Father wads up his paper and throws it in the ashtray. I take it and unfold it: "Certain success in what you are planning."

My sister flips through Al Ahram. She says she wants to see Vivian Leigh in the movie Lady Hamilton.

I steal away to the door leading out of the room. To the right, a wall separates the kitchen from the parlor. The sounds of Saadiya's movements come from the other side of it. To the left there's a door leading to the living room. A dining table between two huge sideboards with a rectangular mirror hanging over it. A large Grundig radio. I walk around the table to the guest room. Its door is closed. I peek through the keyhole. In the darkness, the frame of the doorway leading to the veranda appears. I go around to the bedroom. I open the door and go in. A wide dresser has a headboard made up of three linked mirrors. Next to it is a wooden coat rack covered with clean white cloth. A bed with brass legs. Its bedspread has a lace cover like the one we had in our old house. I head for the mirror next to it. There's a shelf at the bottom of it filled with perfume bottles and jars of cream: Chanel Nº5, Cologne, Atkinson, Max Factor, and a blue bottle like the one my mother had. I touch the bottles and smell their caps.

I go out and close the door softly. I move on to the children's room. I open the door. Two beds facing each other with a small desk next to each. On both there is a colored pen case with a sliding cover and a container holding pens, erasers, and pencil sharpeners. A wide dresser. Everything is organized and clean. A colored cardboard box sits on top of the dresser. *Sister Nabila brings it down and sets it on the rug. She takes several metal sticks out of it. She sets them one after the other to form a circle. She puts the train carriages on top of it. A warning light, two dips in the track, then the station. A staircase with small steps. All the parts are made of shiny colors. There's not a scratch on it. She winds its spring and the train fires out and makes its way around the track while blowing out steam. No touching allowed. The spring is wound again. After two or three rounds, she says: "Enough." She puts everything back into the box and hides it away above the dresser.*

I leave the room and close its door. I go out through the living room door. I cross the parlor to the hallway next to the kitchen. The wooden refrigerator closes in winter and has its pipes packed in ice in summer. I go past it and cross in front of the French-style bathroom. Next to it there is a country-style one. I open its door. I stand on top of its two shining marble foot stands on either side of the opening in the middle. I pee. I leave the bathroom. I close its door after me. I go into the bigger bathroom next to it. It has a French toilet and a shower with a wide drain. I wash my hands and study the things on the shelf of the mirror. Select soap. A case of Gillette razors. A tube of Colinos. Zambuk cream for skin and hair removal. Nolan hair cream. A jar of Brylcreem. I unscrew its cover and dip my finger in. I spread it on my hair and put the cover back on. I study my hair in the mirror. It looks the same as it was. I leave the bathroom and stop near the door to the terrace room.

Father's voice: "Do you see your brother?" My sister's voice: "Rarely? You?" "He's cut me off ever since your blessed mother died and he found out that I remarried." "How's Rowhaya doing?" Father's voice: "Same as always." "And the Turkish woman? What's her name? Basima?" *Her legs are crossed as she sits on the couch covered with colored cloth and I'm next to her. She's white and plump and wears a shiny red dress. Her head is covered with a white scarf. On the wall there's a picture of an important officer with a huge moustache riding a stallion and waving his sword in his hand. She gives me a big piece of chocolate. I peel off its shiny red wrapper with the gold lining and bite off a piece then put it back in its wrapper. I stick it in my jacket pocket. After a while, I take it out and bite off another piece. A hum of voices comes from the guest room. I make out my father's voice and that of another man. The plump woman listens in on the voices with interest. She sees that I'm watching her. She calls the servant woman and tells her to turn on the radio. It sits on a small shelf on the wall facing us, covered with a white cloth. She asks me how old I am. I say: "Nine."She listens to the radio. First talk, then music. I get up the courage to ask: "What's that?" "A movie." "What kind of movie?" "It's called* The Mysterious Past." *I recognize the voice of Laila Murad. She sings: "I wish you were close enough for my eyes to see you ..." I get up and go towards the guest room. Its door with its square glass panels is opened a crack. I listen to the talking. The man's voice: "The boy's too big."My father's voice: "But he studies hard and does what he's told." He comes out. He takes me by the hand and we head towards the door. The plump woman's disappeared, but Laila Murad is still singing.*

Father's voice: "She didn't ask me for a thing. We just went our separate ways."

My sister: "Papa, that's enough marrying for you."

"With God as my witness, I only married her after I'd been ruined by the maids and housekeepers."

"Papa, you know no one can put up with you."

Father asks about Samira, Uncle Fahmi's sister. She says she is busy helping her daughter shop for furniture from Al-Samry Furniture Gallery. She asks him about my uncle. She says he hasn't come round since the last holiday. Their chatting stops for a minute and the sound of the dice clattering down on to the backgammon board resounds. Uncle Fahmi's voice: "It looks like they're closing up the whorehouses." My sister's voice: "And where are the girls supposed to go now?" "They'll head out to the streets."

I walk into the terrace room. The talking stops. I stand next to father. He plays as though he's bored. The game ends with my sister's husband winning. Father closes the backgammon set, saying that it is getting dark and we had better get going. Uncle Fahmi goes out to get a new pack of cigarettes. Father leans over and whispers something to Nabila. She shakes her head. Father stands up. Uncle Fahmi comes back. He urges us to stay and my sister joins in: "Spend the night. Dinner's already ready." *She spreads out a comfy mattress for us on the ground and covers it with a clean sheet that has its own fresh smell. Maybe some rose water mixed in with the detergent. The pillows are soft and clean, not lumpy and rough like our pillows. The quilt is also clean and smells nice. My father wears a gallabiya they've put aside for him. It's perfect and white. As the light stays on, I lie and listen to the soft clatter of the dice on the backgammon board.*

He stands firm on his decision to leave. My sister brings him a small pair of rose-colored pyjama bottoms. "Papa, do you remember these pyjamas? You brought them for me when I was in primary school. I wanted to throw them away at first, but then I said, 'they'll do.'" She brings them over to me and measures them against the side of my leg. She wraps them in newspaper. Father takes them without saying anything. Uncle Fahmy turns on the lights on the stairs.

"Don't be a stranger, papa."

"Good night."

Each floor has its own stair lamp, but the lamp on the ground floor is out. We edge through the dark towards the door to the building. I hear the sound of dogs and cling to father. We go out into the street. The smell of flowers comes from the gardens in the nearby villas. We wait at the tram stop. A car passes slowly. Its driver leans on the woman next to him and kisses her on the mouth. I put my arm against father's leg to make him notice them. "What is it?" I don't answer.

We hear the sound of the tramcar before it appears. It

shoots off with us at a scary speed. The car rocks from side to side. Father is frowning. I hear him muttering. *"My heart is breaking over my son and my son's heart is like a stone."* The stations are all empty so we blow past them without stopping.

At Abbasiya Square we switch to another tram. We get off that one at our square and cross the street. We stop in front of Abdel Malik's French-style bakery. Father buys a bag of stuffed cookies with sesame seeds. We take a side street so that we won't pass in front of the grocer's shop. The quarter is covered in darkness and so is our building. We go into our dark apartment. The lamp in the hallway is burned out. I cling to father's clothes until he can open the door to our room and light the lamp inside. He heats a cup of sugar and water. He puts a tray on top of the bed and we sit next to it. We dip the cookies in the water. He says our house is the best place in the world.

I open my old science notebook. I make sure the feather that was pressed between the pages is still there. I linger over the picture of the hoopoe that I love so much. The electric reading lamp grows dim, like it does every night. I take up the Pharaonic history of Egypt textbook with the blue cover. I flip through the pages, looking at the pictures. Menes of the two kingdoms. Father finishes the evening prayer on top of the bed. He gets down. He pulls the woolen cap down all the way over his head to his neck. He wraps his robe around his body. He makes two tight fists and shoves them down into his pockets. He paces the room backwards and forwards. He is "taking a stroll," as he says when he explains how important it is after eating dinner.

I complain about the cold. He brings the primus stove from the living area, lights it, and sets it near the edge of the rug. The covering of my notebook is torn. I ask him to make it a new cover. I hand him some yellow cover paper. I bring him the scissors but he refuses to use them. He sits on the edge of the bed, folds the paper, and passes over it with his fingers several times. Then he carefully tears it at the crease. He divides the paper into two equal halves with no sign of cutting at their edges. He sets one of them aside, then puts the book in the center of the other. He folds the paper inside the front cover of the book, then overlays its top edge. He sticks it between the paper and the cover. He repeats the same thing with the bottom flap, then moves on to the back cover and does the same thing.

There is a knock at the door of the room. I open it for Uncle Kareem, the constable. He is wearing a black military overcoat on top of a white *gallabiya*. He has a thick moustache that stretches across his upper lip. Father welcomes him and nods for him to sit down on the edge of the bed. I go back to my desk. He has his back to me. I can smell that odor of his military overcoat that I like so much. Father sits with his legs crossed on top of the bed. He turns his body a little until he is facing both the constable and me. He rests his back against the headboard of the bed.

The constable takes a pack of Hollywood cigarettes out of his pocket. He offers one to father, but he declines. Instead, he gets out his own box of black cigarettes. It has a yellow wrapper with a red Abyssinian head in the middle of it. The constable lights a match and extends his hand. Father tilts his head forward, moving his cigarette close to the flame. He holds the tip in the flame until it starts to glow. I bring over the ashtray from the desk and put it down on the bedspread between the two of them. The constable crosses his legs, locks his fingers, and wraps his hands around his knees. A gold watch flashes from his wrist.

He looks around, then says: "Don't you have a radio?"

"It's being fixed."

I know it's not true. Father sold it a long time ago. The constable goes on as though he doesn't believe father: "There's a Philips radio that only costs 12 pounds."

"So it costs a month's salary?"

"You can pay it in installments."

He suggests to father that they play a round of dominoes. He pulls a handful of evenly cut clippings of thick grey paper out of his pocket. Father straightens out the covers. He pulls up the long head pillow, folds it, and puts it between himself, and the young man. He asks me to bring his glasses from on top of the desk. Kareem puts the papers on top of the pillow. Father picks up one and studies it. The constable says they are tickets from the train he takes to visit his mother. He shuffles the tickets together like playing cards and puts them on top of the pillow. Each of them picks up seven of the strips of paper. Father rests his cigarette at the edge of the ashtray. He lines them up on the palm of his hands and slants them up in order to keep them out of the other man's sight. The constable does the same thing. He takes out a paper and puts it down in the middle of the pillow. He says: "Double ones."

Father notices that I'm watching the game and scolds me. He tells me to finish my homework and get my satchel ready. When one of the domino papers falls to the floor, I run to grab it for them. The words "From Al-Mattareya to Lemon Bridge" are written in black letters on one side. On the other side, little circles have been drawn and filled in with a copying pencil. To the side, the ticket puncher's mark takes the shape of a small triangle.

Father picks out one of his tickets. He puts it by the pair of fives, saying: "Double twos." The constable plays one of his. Father has to draw from the stack of papers. He tells the story about the spider we found in the toilet. Kareem says that they like to sneak into the warm places in the body, especially between the legs or under the knees. It hides there until it's warmed up, then it bites and kills. Father says it's just a particular type of spider and it is harmless, and then he throws in: "The apartment has to be painted."

The young man says: "Or you could look for another place."

"I'm right there with you ... but where? We thought housing would be cheaper after the English left Cairo. Instead, prices are on fire."

"Sir, have you heard of the Waqf Ministry's low-cost housing projects?"

"Yes. The ministry limited the rent of a single room in them to five pounds. That means the whole flat could go up to twenty or thirty pounds a month. So what is the clerk who only makes ten or fifteen pounds a month supposed to do?"

"Double fours and one! I'll talk to Hajj Abdel Razik for you."

"Who's that?"

"He's a big trader in the scrap metal market in Boulak. He's constructing a building at the end of Nuzha Street."

He tells him that he started out as a traveling salesman of bottles. Before the war, he made a pact with a drug company to supply it with ten thousand empty medicine bottles. One sold for two millimes. He was going to make ten pounds out of the whole deal, but suddenly the war broke out and the company tore up the agreement. He had to work in English army camps. After the war, the cost of everything rose and the price of an empty bottle hit four piastres. He sold his whole stock to a brewery for 400 pounds and came out with a tidy sum.

Father says: "Everyone's making money like its growing on trees."

The constable shakes his head. He says that luck needs pluck and that he knows someone who bought salvage items from the British camp for a hundred thousand pounds. One of the things he got was huge iron barrels. When he opened them, he found them filled with car tires that he turned around and sold for fifty thousand pounds.

I cough harshly. Father gets up and goes to the door of the balcony to crack it open so some of the cigarette smoke can escape. Kareem says that people are forming co-ops now with several members, where each one pays a certain amount every month, and they all pool their resources. Father keeps quiet and says nothing.

The constable mixes up the domino papers and puts them down on the pillow: "If you have anything left over from your sugar coupons or the ones for eighteen liters of oil, I am ready to buy them." *The math teacher yells at me: "Stretch out your hands." I unfold my cold hands with their palms facing down. He raises the ruler in the air, then swings it down with its edge across the back of my hand. I tell him I've brought kerosene coupons with me. He pulls the ruler back.*

A commotion in the neighborhood. Screams, from more than one person. The noise dies down after a while. The constable says: "That's the guy who has two wives."

Father asks about the neighbors from the balcony facing ours. The constable says it's a medical student living with his two sisters, who spend all their time on the balcony waiting for Mr. Right.

"And the girls at the first house on the street?"

'They're the children of Sabri Effendi, the clerk in the Justice Ministry. The oldest one is named Siham. She's always standing in the window. She's waiting for Mr. Right too."

"What about the woman up above us?"

"She's hot, don't you think? She's a nurse. Seems to be a widow or a divorcée. She lives alone with her little son."

Father says: "If only I could find a nice young lady that could put up with my crustiness and raise the boy for me. I'm tired of the maids and cooking ladies."

"And you'd marry her?"

"Yeah, as long as she couldn't have children."

"I might be able to find you someone back in my hometown." *I fight violently with the cooking lady's son. Basima treats him as though he's her son. I wait in the morning until she leaves the bedroom and goes to the bathroom. I go in to complain to my father. He stands next to the bed and fastens his hernia belt. His face is in a frown. On the night stand next to the bed there is a small bottle with a picture of a lion on it.*

The constable leaves the room and comes back with a section of cloth and two pairs of pyjamas. The cloth is thick and dark brown. Father says as he studies it: "Is this cloth for curtains?" The constable says: "It could work for a suit." He unfolds the two pyjamas. One is white with stripes and shiny metal buttons. Father says: "This is for prisoners of war." He tells me to try them on. They fit me. The other pair is pale yellow with buttons from mother of pearl. He says they're lighter

54

and can be worn in summer. Father tells him to bring them back on the first of the month.

The constable acts all pleasant: "Don't worry about the money." Father puts the cloth and two pairs of pyjamas to the side. The constable says: "I also have nylon stockings for women." Father laughs: "See anyone in this room who could wear them?"

He puts a cup of water on top of the desk. From the drawer he takes the mirror with the cracked metal frame and the small shaving box that holds his razor blades. He sets both on the desk and sits down behind it. He dips the brush with the wooden handle, whose coating is peeling off, into the water. He scrapes it across a block of soap with a silver wrapper in the shape of a fat candle. I ask if he's planning to go out, but he doesn't answer. He paints over his beard several times until it turns into a big cloud of foam. He takes the purple packaging off the razor. He brushes its edge back and forth against his fat palm and then puts it in the metal shaver. He scrapes it across his cheek then dips it in the cup of water to wash away the soap. He does this many times. His cheeks turn smooth like silk. He takes the colored towel from the edge of the bed and wipes the last traces of soap from his face. He stands straight up and starts to put on his clothes. He takes out his blue suit. He pulls its braces over his shoulders. He puts on the matching waistcoat with the back made from black silk cloth. Its buckle straps that fasten around the middle dangle from either side. He turns his back to me so he can fasten the two straps. I play up to him to try to get him to take me along. He refuses: "No. You have homework." He points to the desk. "Sit there and don't get up. I won't be long."

He brushes the surface of his fez with the sleeve of his suit coat. He twists the two sides of his moustache all the way up to his nostrils then lets them loose. He brushes them with his fingers. He opens the glass inner doors of the balcony and takes hold of the wooden shutter doors by their side hooks. He pushes them open and fastens them in place with the hooks. He closes the glass doors again. I ask him to close the door of the room when he leaves, and I listen to the sound of him shutting the door to the apartment and to his lazy steps on the outer stairs.

The sound of his feet grows distant. I leave the chair at my desk. I throw off the blanket that I've wrapped around myself. I pull the door of the dresser open a crack. I look through the clothes that are all scattered and messed up. I drag over the desk chair and stand on it. I see the book shoved against the side of the top shelf. The constable brought it, and right away I wanted to look at it, but father scolded me. It's a small book in a foreign language. Folded across two pages of it is a statue of a naked woman. The name "Venus" appears in the caption. I flip through the rest of the pages and put it back in its place.

I study the other things on the shelf. Bottles of medicine. A fine glass tube with a red label: Carter Pills, to aid digestion. Belmonks for coughs. A bottle of Aspro brand aspirin. Brockton Drops. Half a piece of nutmeg. Father puts a dash under his tongue whenever he drinks a cup of coffee. A jar filled with bicarbonate of soda powder. He dissolves it in water and takes whiffs from it. A tattered doll from the holiday fair on the prophet's birthday. Another plastic bottle with two pieces of black dried prune. Father uses it when he can't go. A book with a colored cover called *The Queen's Messenger.* The inside page has an ad for "Zayiz brand Armchairs" and another for "Otter Brandy." Cupping glasses stacked on top of each other. A big government notebook full of journal entries written by mother. *She writes large round letters in it with a pencil. She finishes on a line and then skips the next line and writes some more. She reads out some of what she has written to father. I hear the names "Hitler," "Gandhi," and "Miles Lampson."*

A small can with several identity cards that have father's name on them. The title "Bey" doesn't appear after his name. He says that it is only written with the first rank beys and that he is only a second rank one. Two old pictures, the size of post-cards. The first one has a grey border around an oval frame. Inside is a child wearing a long embroidered dress and white sandals. A white towel hangs around his neck and dangles at his chest. He's standing near the top of a flight of stairs. His hand is clutching a stone railing and it's hard to make out the details of his face. I turn it over. On the back is my full name with the name of father, written in my mother's hand.

The other picture has my father sitting wearing a fez and a tie. Between his knees a small child wearing a two-piece shorts suit is standing. Its first piece starts at the neck, and its second goes all the way down to the knees. The picture is in black and white, except for the child's clothes. The suit is a blue-green color with two yellow stripes around the wrists and around the waist. On the back, there's my name and father's name too.

The handwriting is my mother's.

I search in the rest of the drawers. A book called *The Family Doctor.* I flip through the pages. Twisted faces on a torn page. Another book about high prayer has the fatiha in it and some prayers of supplication. Alboosiry's *The Prophet's Cloak. Things of Merit and Their Opposites* by Al-Jahiz. A page is dog-eared. At the top of it there's a title in bold: "The Glories of Marriage." An issue of the magazine *Pocket Chat.* On the top cover is a colored picture of a beautiful foreign actress. In the corner, there's a circle around the price: 20 millimes. I throw it on top of the bed. A huge book has white strips of paper dangling from the sides of some of its pages. I take it and climb down.

I lie down on the bed and roll over on the covers. I flip through the pages of the magazine. A picture of a woman shows her from the back wearing nothing but small under-pants. I stop for a while at the cartoons. Most of them are about men with big bellies smoking cigars. War profiteers. A drawing of two men with a caption that reads: "At the Indus-trial Agricultural Exposition." One of them says: "How could you bring your mother-in-law to the exposition?" The second says: "I told myself bring her. God is generous. Maybe he'll bless us and she'll get lost in the crowd."

One says to another: "Prices are on fire. Come on, let's warm ourselves."

I throw the magazine to one side and take up the huge book. *The Great Star of Knowledge.* Its pages are yellow. There is a dark block print in the middle of the page and all around it. It's hard to make out the letters. There are circles and squares divided into columns and joined to form numbers and words. I open up to the pages with the white strips dangling from them. How to achieve compromise between man and wife. How to increase income. How to overcome forgetfulness. How to live a long life. How to expel insects from the house. How to increase understanding and memorization. To restore eyesight. To suppress desire. To accumulate wealth without effort. To disappear in front of human eyes. To fulfill one's needs and stand before high officials. For the slow learner to overcome his problems in comprehension and memorization.

I close the book and put both it and the magazine back in their place in the drawer. I take out the small brass kettle from under the bed. I spoon out a little bit of sugar and half the bag of chickpeas. I sit with my legs crossed at the edge of the rug near the door. I put the kettle in front of me on the bare floor. I crush the mixture with the handle of the kettle. I keep crushing it until it turns into a smooth yellow paste. I get rid of a clump of it that sticks to the handle. Then I remember the spoons are all in the living area. I look at the closed door. I hold the kettle in my hands and dip a finger in to eat from it.

I stop behind the door of the balcony. A fenugreek seed has been planted there in a cup. A thin green stalk has sprouted from it and sways in the wind. The balcony across from us is lit up. The curtains are open but the glass doors are shut. One of the two sisters stares out at me from behind them. Um Safwat comes out from the door of the house. She is tall and light-skinned. Her hair is uncovered. It is smooth and she has had it cut short. She wears a colored scarf around her neck. Her face has been powdered. Her son is trailing behind her. He's about my age. He is wearing a clean, pressed suit. He walks with head bowed. She's screaming at him.

I pull back from the cold. I set the kettle on top of the table. I take a tangerine. I peel it and then toss the peel and seeds underneath the bed. I bend over and pull out the large suitcase with the battered side. I lift the top part. Inside, it is lined with blue paper. Books with tattered pages. Some of them have been scribbled over with pencil. One book has a scary colored cover and the title, *The Abandoned Castle*. A thin, webbing army belt, drab olive in color with a brass buckle, is used for tying up the suitcase when it's stored. An old check register. A gas mask. Small pieces of pencil. Empty match boxes. Ashtrays made of porcelain. *The small statues behind the closed glass doors of the small cupboard. A round tray of colored porcelain with Japanese drawings. Another's in the shape of a rectangle and forms a metal shield with holes in it. I put it in front of me on the rug. I push it along and take turns whistling once like a train, once like a car horn. I line up the chairs of the dining table in a row. I hang the ticket collector's bag over my shoulder. The ticket book is in my hand. My father made it from colored paper that he fastened into a book with cardboard and string.*

I put the top back down. I take out the ships made of paper. Father has put them together with skill and ease. I carry them to the bed and stack them up. The small ships first, then the big ocean liners. I divide them into two groups face to face. Each group has its own lead vessel that you can tell from the match stick coming out of the front. The two groups go to battle and some of the ships are hit and fall over on their side. I get bored after a while.

There's a wrapper full of Egyptian Romano cheese and another with local pastrami on the table. I tear off half a loaf of bread, and put a slice of pastrami in it. The voices of neighborhood children in the streets come through. I rush to the balcony. Children my age and younger cling to each other by their clothes, as they form a train that moves through the quarter. Their voices rise: "Throw in that coal and steam the train along." They form a ring and one of them stands to the side. He calls out: "The fox." They call out together in one voice: "It's gone. Gone." "What about its tail?" "Seven turns." "And the lady bear?" "It fell down the well." "And it's owner?" "A big fat pig." "Did the wolf get by you, the Sahlawi wolf?" "It's gone. Gone." *He looks from the window in his square white cap, smoking a black cigarette. Cops and robbers. I play with them bravely; I'm not afraid of the others.*

The voice of Ragaa Abdou comes from Um Zakiya's radio. The sun goes down. I turn on the electric lantern. The blanket is cold. The wind rattles the door to the balcony. I take down a book in French from the row of Nabila's school textbooks. I flip through the pages. A drawing of a man in the rain. He is covered by a wide cloak and holds an umbrella over his head. An empty street. A boat. I listen carefully.

The fall of heavy steps echoes out on the staircase. The steps stop in front of our apartment, then they continue upwards.

When is papa coming? Coming at six o'clock!

Walking or riding? Riding down the block!

He appears at the door of the apartment in his full suit with fez and carrying a paper bag in his left hand. His dark face is beaming. He leans over towards me and takes me in his arms. He kisses me on each cheek and then buries his mouth against my neck. I pull back my face to avoid his prickly moustache. I say to him: "Papa, let go." He tickles my chin with his finger saying: "Put on your little duckling hat, chin of the kitty cat."

Finally, his steps fall. They come up slowly as the shoes scrape across the stairs. I hear the sound of the key turning the lock of the outer door. He opens the door to our room. He comes in and turns around: "Come in, Um Muhammad." A tall woman, so thin it's scary, wrapped in one of the flowing black cloaks of the countryside, walks in. Her hair is covered by a black shawl. Her face is sun baked and covered with wrinkles. A long nose. Narrow eyes. She carries a big bundle under her arm. She stands in the middle of the room. He invites her to sit on the edge of the bed. She sits down, keeping her two feet flat on the floor. Black stockings and very old black shoes with low heels. She sets the bundle next to her on the bed. She won't look at either one of us.

Father takes off his overcoat and hangs it on the rack. He says to her: "Come along so I can show you the apartment and let you change your clothes." She takes her bundle in her hand and follows him to the living room.

"The toilet's there. Its door doesn't close all the way. The toilet is broken. You can change your clothes in the guest room."

He leaves her and comes back. He takes off his jacket and puts a robe on over his waistcoat and slacks. He leans over the bed. He takes out a bag of vermicelli and a jar of sugar. "Do you want some vermicelli with milk?" I don't answer. When he leaves the room, I hear the muffled sound of the stove, then the rustling of the fire. The sizzle of the butter. He comes back after a while scowling. "The milk's gone bad." Um Muhammad comes in wearing a black dress. She is wearing thick black socks and the bundle is still under her arm. She puts it on the bed and sits on the edge. From the bundle she pulls a miniature pack of cigarettes and takes out a flat one. Father wrinkles his brow. He hands her a box of matches without saying anything. She lights her cigarette. Father brings the pot of vermicelli. She says she's not hungry. He and I eat it with just sugar since there is no milk.

He suggests that she stretch out on the bed if she's tired. She doesn't answer. He tells her: "Um Muhammad, you and I are fully married according to God's law and the order established by His prophet." She stands straight up, then climbs on to the bed. She takes over my place next to the wall. When I set myself down next to her, I smell a strong odor of dirt or mud. Her legs knock against the frame of the bed. She folds them up and her hard knees knock against me. I move away from her toward the edge of the bed. Father turns off the light and lies down next to me. I cling to him, surrounding him with my arms.

Chapter Two

Maged Effendi shows up in the doorway of the shop. He wears a three-piece suit with no overcoat. His suit is neatly pressed. His face shines in the light of the electric lamp. His sunken forehead has a line of carefully combed, black hair at the top. His ears stick out. Everyone welcomes him in. Abdel 'Alim cries out: "Welcome to the groom!" The groom smiles proudly. Father asks him: "Did you really marry a genie?" He pulls me by my arm to let him have the chair I'm in. I stand between father's knees as Maged Effendi sits in my place.

Everyone's eyes are fixed on him. The turbaned sheikh is there in his jubbah and caftan. So is Refaat Effendi with a copy of today's *Al-Masri* folded up in his hand. Father asks again: "How are things?" Maged Effendi thinks for a second, then says: "Like any marriage." Abdel 'Alim cries out: "Are you kidding? Tell us all about it. But first, what are you drinking?" "Fenugreek tea, with milk." Abdel 'Alim calls to Abbas, who is standing on the porch of the shop and tells him to bring fenugreek.

Maged Effendi says that she was the one who had asked him to marry her, but on the condition that he never take a second wife and that he never eat garlic or onion at night. Father comments: "She's right on that point." Maged Effendi keeps going and says that he has to admit she has her good points. She helps him out with money when he's short and when he comes back home at the end of the day, she has dinner ready for him, including all kinds of fruit, even if they're not in season. The house stays clean, and his clothes are always washed.

"So what are you mad about?"

He says he cannot control her, that she pops up whenever he thinks of her, then just as suddenly, disappears whenever she feels like it. She reads his mind before he even has a thought, making it impossible to keep any kind of secret from her.

The fenugreek tea arrives and he takes a sip. Abdel 'Alim leans over and whispers in his ear. He answers back: "Beyond your wildest dreams." Then he turns to everyone and says: "She does whatever it takes to make me happy and keep me from getting tired of her." Some nights, she even asks him what type of woman he wants, then she takes that shape on to herself. This time a blonde foreigner in a bikini, that time a belly dancer that looks just like Tahia Karioka, and the next time in a short tartan skirt, like a student just back from school.

Silence surrounds the group. A woman comes in wearing a black wrap. She turns her back to us and asks Saleem for 50 dirham worth of halva. Everyone turns around to look at her. Her wrap clings tightly around her and the lower part of her leg shows from underneath it. Father's look fixes on her full, bare calf. He loosens his coat and puts his hand in the watch pocket of his waistcoat. He lifts his left hand to his mouth and brushes his finger across his moustache as he exchanges a smile with Hajj Abdel 'Alim.

Maged Effendi pushes himself to his feet: "Pardon me, everyone. I have to go before she calls me." He leaves the shop in a hurry. I take back my chair. The turbaned sheikh says: "Real girls can't find husbands anywhere, and he goes and marries a genie." Refaat unfolds his copy of *Al-Masri*. He flips through its pages, then sees something and stops. "Listen to what Duriya Shafiq is writing: 'The danger of spinsterhood is haunting the young women of Egypt because its men are on strike against marriage.'" The sheikh says: "That woman has gone too far. Ladies are crowding men out of jobs. The last straw is that girls from good families are being hired as airline stewardesses."

Hajj Abdel 'Alim leans over to father and whispers something. Father answers back: "She just won't do. The whole time she sits on the balcony holding a Coutarelli cigarette. She can't cook or clean. She gets a jar of water and throws it on the floor and that's that. She thinks she's still out in the countryside, throwing water around to get the dust to settle." A minute later, he adds: "Today I yelled at her. She sat there jabbering all day. I couldn't understand a damn thing."

Abdel 'Alim suggests we all go outside because the shop has become stuffy. Abbas takes our chairs and lines them up on the pavement near the entrance. The light thrown across from the chemist's shop sparkles around us. I get a half-piastre from father and go over to the shop to buy a Robson, a round piece of liquorice-flavored sweet with a blue chickpea in the middle.

When I get back, I find Dr. Aziz in my seat. His huge belly hangs over the top of his trousers. I stand between father's knees. The doctor asks me about school. Father complains to him that I'm a picky eater. The doctor suggests that I drink

Ovaltine and take vitamins. Father says: "I'm sick too. I have dizzy spells and I can't get up from the bed."

"Come by my clinic and I'll take your blood pressure."

Father asks Hajj Abdel 'Alim about the landlord's promise to unlock the public toilet and let people use it. Abdel 'Alim says that he has spoken with them but it hasn't done any good. He adds: "Why don't you go use the *hammam* in Al Husseiniya?" The turbaned sheikh shakes his head: "Respectable people don't go there. Don't all of you know about what goes on there?"

A fat priest wearing black robes comes up and joins us. His head is covered with something that looks like a plate with dark cloth wrapped tightly around it. He asks Refaat: "Has anyone read the new poem by al-Aqqad?" Father asks: "What's it about?" "He sings the praises of the lips of the actress Camilia, the one that Akhbar al-Youm calls 'the warm mouth.'" Dr. Aziz says that she has become the king's mistress. Hajj Abdel 'Alim says: "Poor Queen Fareeda." Refaat says that there was a watermelon seller calling out to the passers-by: "Royal watermelons!" Someone buys one, and the seller splits it open for him, it turns out to be a pumpkin, at which the seller explains: "Royal—King Farouk—watermelons." Everyone laughs and I realize that it's a joke.

I leave my place and turn around so that I'm behind Dr. Aziz. I look down at the newspaper in his hand. There's a picture of an open police van with several young men inside being guarded by soldiers. The van is moving down the middle of the street. A Sawaris car being pulled by two donkeys tilts to the side. Refaat Effendi says: "The trials of Hussein Tawfiq and Anwar Sadat are almost over. After that, it'll be the communist's turn."

He reads one of the headlines on the side columns: "The Egyptian Government Takes over the al-Qantara to Haifa Rail Line from the English." I pull my head away when he folds up the newspaper. I peek inside the upper pocket of his suit coat where he keeps a white handkerchief. He has an uncovered fountain pen in it and there's a huge ink spot on the end of the handkerchief. He says in an annoyed tone of voice: "The Jews are getting ready to fight, and we're in our own little world. The government goes on its winter break then starts planning for summer vacation, and the leaders keep talking about something they call 'positive steps,' but none of us has a clue what 'positive steps' means in the first place."

Hajj Abdel 'Alim lets out an "ahem." He says that people have lost trust in the political parties and their leaders.

Refaat Effendi gets ready to defend the Wafd Party and its leader, Mustafa al-Nahas. Father turns to him and says that he wrote a letter of complaint about the way social security payments were disbursed and sent it to *Al Ahram,* but they didn't publish it. He explains that he took a big advance from his retirement money under a plan in which he could pay back the advance in monthly payments. Now the advance is all paid back and they're still taking the payments. "It's worse than usury. I'm thinking about suing the government." The lawyer asks him: "When you asked for the advance, did you know that they'd keep taking payments out forever?" Father says that he needed the money badly at the time. Then the lawyer speaks in a decisive voice: "It's a contractual agreement between you and the government. You agreed to their conditions. The contract is legitimized by the parties." He crosses his legs, then adds: "Anyway, we can make a claim on the basis that the contract is punitive."

Father turns to the priest: "Tell us, your holiness, when do we get out the Ouija board?" *They sit around rocks made into a circle on the ground. Inside, there are triangles, squares, and strange words. The priest reads in a raised voice from a book as they watch the shapes. Father passes dishes of rice pudding around.*

The turbaned sheikh makes a show of his anger. Hajj Abdel 'Alim turns to him: "God gave our lord Solomon use of the djinn. We're just going to speak with djinn that are Muslim believers. We're not asking for anything that'll corrupt us either. We just want it to raise the treasure hiding under the earth's surface up for us."

Father talks about what happened when he called on the servant of the "Latif,' or holy God. He made a habit of doing it every night. Finally, he heard a bump in the living room over the sideboard, and an angry voice came to him: "What do you want?" And he was so scared that he didn't answer, so the servant never came back after that.

Dr. Aziz says good-bye and gets up to leave. Hajj Adbel 'Alim asks him: "Are you planning on listening to the Um Kalthoum concert?" Father asks what her new song is about. The Hajj answers him: "It's called 'I Could not have a Generous Heart.'" The doctor says he will listen to the concert at home.

They chat about Hajj Mishaal. Abdel 'Alim says that he sits around counting out 100 pound banknotes the way ordinary people count change out from small bills. The turbaned sheikh adds that he traded in people's salvage goods before the war.

The fruitseller who walks around the quarter passes by. He calls out that he has oranges from Jaffa. Father buys two *okas'* worth. He tells Refaat Effendi: "Who knows when we'll see these again?" We get up after a while. The entrance to the house is dark, as always. Our apartment too. There is a faint light at the entrance to the storage room, like the glow from a candle or an oil lamp. Father knocks on the door. He takes out the key and opens it. The door to our room is open, but the room is pitch black. He calls out: "Um Muhammad!" but she doesn't answer. He calls her again. I hang on to his clothes. We go into the room and he turns on the light. He comes back out. I follow him. He wanders through the nooks and crannies of the apartment, calling out: "Um Muhammad." There is no sign of her. We go back to our room. He looks around for her bundle and cannot find it. He says: "The old crone has taken off."

He looks through the dresser trying to make sure she hasn't stolen anything. I sit down at my desk and open up my composition notebook. A visit to the zoological gardens. *Hassan the sea lion. Cheetah the monkey. Sayyid Qishta the hippo. Mother wears a light coat over a patterned dress. We walk over paths of colored pebbles. We sit down at the tea stall. Suddenly, mother jumps up, saying: "We have to get away from here. We have to go back now." My father tries to calm her. She keeps repeating: "Something terrible is going to happen. We have to go back the way we came."*

notebook filled with thick paper. He throws himself into his drawing.

I take out my pencil and sharpener and open up my notebook. *We walk downhill until we get to the florist's shop, then we stroll towards the square. We cross it and stand on the sidewalk in the middle of the crowd waiting for the grand procession. If we get lucky, we'll see the king in his red convertible.*

I draw a camel. It looks more like a donkey. I try to erase it, but its lines are still visible on the page. I get up and look for Maher, but I can't find him. The teacher is still absorbed in his drawing. He seems not to know that we are there. One of the students goes up to him and asks for help. The teacher answers him then fills his page with quick line drawings. The student goes back to his seat. He puts the notebook in his satchel, picks it up and, heading towards the door of the class, sneaks out.

I put the sharpener on the point of the pencil and turn it several times. The point sharpens, then breaks off. I sharpen it again. Another student wants help from the teacher. A third one follows him. A fourth and a fifth. Each of them leaves the class after he does their drawing for them. After a while, our numbers dwindle until I find myself sitting alone. I take my notebook and go to him. I put it in front of him without a word. He neither looks at me, nor speaks to me. He draws a camel bending down with one stroke of the pen. I steal a glance at his notebook. Country houses in a row. Their fronts are drawn with careful detail. I go back to my seat. I put the notebook in my satchel, pick it up, and head towards the door. I turn around to look at him. He is absorbed in his drawing.

We scatter at the front door of the school. A sky full of

clouds warns of rain. The breeze smells nice. The pavement made of colored gravel. The wall surrounding the Jewish school. A colored poster advertises the film *Sanity Takes a Vacation*, starring Mohamed Fawzi, Layla Fawzi, Bishara Wakeem, Abdel Salaam al-Nabulsi. The film *Bol-bol Effendi* is playing at the Corsal cinema with Sabah and Fareed al-Atrash.

I walk beside the wall of the school until I come to the corner. The tall windows are open. I look down over tables set up in messy rows, with grains of wheat scattered on top of them. A strange smell. A few steps and I find myself in front of our old house. The clouds part the way for bright sunshine. The iron door is closed. The windows are closed. *Mother gets up and goes out to nurse my sister. My father wears a robe over his* gallabiya, *and he has replaced his nightcap with a fez. He goes along with me to the road. We walk along the quiet street. We pass a monk wearing a white outfit. His pale face is sunburned. My father winks at him and stammers in French: Coamantalleefu? We go about half way up the street, then turn back. I walk close to the wall of the garden of the convent school with its thick trees. I steal a look inside. My father stands waiting for me. I know he's watching me. I pretend to be all wrapped up in watching what's around me. The light of dusk starts to break up. He calls to me in a commanding voice.*

I cross the street. I stand under one of the two windows. One is the bedroom window, the other the dining room. Next to it is the alleyway, which the window of the guest room and the steel-grated kitchen window look down on to. The alleyway ends at the storage house for the barrels of molasses. That's why the yellow-striped hornets gather there. *One of the children manages to catch one of them. He ties its stinger with a thread.*

77

A private car with an arched roof comes by, moving up from the part of the street that dead ends into the square. It heads down a side street that goes toward the shanty town. It stops in front of the villa a few doors down from our house. A plump man gets out wearing clothes of the countryside underneath a loose-fitting *aba. The same man is in a white jacket, blue trousers, and white shoes, with a strikingly beautiful woman in a green dress, on his arm. There's a sunken spot at her temple near her ear. My father says that it's the remains of a green tattoo that peasants have. The two of them come out of the door of the villa. The children and I stand on the pavement across the street. We try to sneak a look inside the villa. There's a small circular garden with cactus plants rising up out of it.*

The sun disappears. Three fat monks pass by in dark brown cloaks. Around each of their waists, there is a long rope, tied in front, with the ends dangling. A cart moves along carrying spools of paper. Two fat nuns in white clothes. A horse-drawn cart. *We run behind it shouting at the driver: Mr. Love Juice. He raises his whip and tries to strike us, as he insults our parents. We notice a boy and a girl walking together under the trees. We yell at them: "Mr. Young Buck, leave the doe alone."*

I know that I'm late and I'll find father mad and waiting for me on the balcony. He'll scold me for tearing the collar of my suit jacket, then we will sit together and eat leftovers. Then he will go to work in the kitchen and leave me alone, sitting behind my desk. Before long, the night will take over without me having enough time to get my homework done.

I start walking again without much enthusiasm. I go out to the square and I cross it. I stop in front of a poster advertising a special screening for students of the film *The Conquest of Egypt,* at the Cosmo cinema. *The Rich and the Famous* at the Majestic, starring Mohamed Abdel Mutlub, Ali al-Kissar, Haggir Hamdi, Abdel Fatah al-Qusari, and Ismail Yasseen.

I enter the alley. I notice father in front of the house across the street talking to its doorman. He waves at me to go inside the house. Abbas sits at the entrance on the steps next to his regular bottle of cheap red whisky. I walk around him trying to keep away from his putrid smell. I go inside the house. The sound of a radio. Abdel Wahab is singing "The wheat tonight, on the night of its harvest."

His voice filters out from inside the apartment. The door is open. The light in the hall is on. The washing line is hanging from the top of the constable's door to the top of the door to the living-room. A short woman with light-colored skin and bare arms hangs up wet clothes while she sings along with the radio. The hall is clean. The tablecloth on the dining table is washed. The top of the sideboard is shiny. The door of our room is open a crack. I go in and put my satchel on the desk. I go to the glass doors to the balcony. Father is still talking to the doorman. He leaves him and heads towards our house. I hear the sound of his careful steps on the stairs outside. He closes the door to the apartment behind him. He comes into the room. Closes the door. I ask about the woman who is hanging the laundry. He says she's the constable's wife.

He comes over to the balcony and stands next to me. He studies the house across from us. Lights a cigarette. He walks back to the door of the room. Returns again to the balcony. After a while, the doorman appears at the entrance of the doorway across the street. He crosses the alley and comes towards our building. Father goes to the door of the room. Opens it a crack. He waits a while until he hears knocking at the door of the apartment. He goes out to open it. I move towards the door that has been left open. I stretch my head out, being careful that he does not see me. I can see him whispering with the doorman. He gives him money and turns to come back to the room. I rush to my desk. Father comes in and says that the neighbors on the balcony across from ours want to see me.

I leave the apartment. I cross the alley. The entrance to the building is dark. The doorman indicates the door at the top of the first flight of steps. I knock on it. Hekmet opens the door. She is tall and heavy and wears a rose-colored light robe over a nightshirt. Her hair is long. Her face is smiling. She has smeared her mouth with lipstick. She gives me a hug and pulls me inside the apartment. Sound of a door slamming shut. Her brother, or her little sister? The cramped living area is cluttered with furniture. She sits me down in an armchair covered with white cloth. A medium-sized radio is on top of the sideboard. The voice of Ismahan sings: "I went once into a garden; I smelt the aroma of flowers."

She sits across from me and asks me my name. She wants to know how old I am and how I like school. I answer all her questions. She asks about my mother. I don't say anything. She asks if I have brothers or sisters. I say: "Two sisters and a brother." She asks about the two sisters and I tell her the older one is married.

"And the younger one?"

"She died a long time ago."

"And your brother?"

"He's grown up."

"Where is he?"

"At his house. See, he's married."

She offers me a sweet. She asks me if I would like something to eat. I shake my head. She brings me a cookie. She insists that I eat it. She watches me with a smile. I finish the cookie and I stand up. She asks me to stay for a while. I tell her I have homework. I head towards the door. She asks me how I'm going to spend Shem al-Naseem, the spring holiday. *The house is full of lettuce and green chickpeas. My father hangs a bow tie made of a green onion stalk on the mantle of the bed. He wakes us in the morning with an onion that he uses to tickle our nose.*

She invites me to come along with her and her brother and sister to the zoo. I say: "I don't know. I have to ask papa."

He tries to get me to eat another stuffed cabbage leaf. I don't like it. I pull my mouth away from his hand as it holds the piece. He says: "There's a roll left. Eat it so we can take the plate back." We pay the constable's wife to leave us part of what she cooks for him. I say no. He eats the remaining roll. Takes the tray back to the kitchen. He comes back after he has washed it, shaking the water off on to the floor. After drying it with a towel, he gives it to me and says: "Don't you dare drop it." I take it and go out to the living room. I knock on the constable's door. The light of the electric lamp shines from underneath it. I knock on it again and call out: "It's me, Mrs. Tahiya."

She opens the door for me with a smile. She has a white silk robe on, fastened with a tasseled belt around the waist. The smell of cigarettes. My eyes sneak a glance behind her. No one is there. The covering of the narrow bed is unmade. Is it wide enough for both of them? To the right, a chiffonier made up of several drawers has a large mirror hung on the wall over it. There's a crack near the top of it. She takes the plate from me. The blood rushes to my face.

I run back to our room. I sit at my desk and solve my math homework problems. I feel hot and have a hard time swallowing. Father touches my forehead. He brings me a cup of water. I try to turn away but firmly he orders me to open my mouth. I swallow the aspirin tablet. He wraps a handkerchief over my collar around my swollen tonsils. He goes with me to the toilet to pee. The door to the constable's room is closed. The sound of the radio comes out from behind it. We go back to the room. He helps me lie down on the bed. He wraps the covers carefully around me and tells me not to worry because he will solve the math problems for me.

I doze off then wake up again. I see him facing me, resting his back against the headboard of the bed. His glasses are sliding down his nose and the math notebook is in his hand. On top of his head there's a square white cap. I nod off again.

I wake up to a booming voice. It is Ali Safa, a friend of father's. He carries in his hand a short, shiny-brown, wooden cane with a patch of leather on the end. He wears a brown suit. Tufts of snow-white hair appear from under the edge of his fez. He cries out: "Is that the same Khalil I used to know? Impossible! Get up old man, and let's go out. There's a hopping poker party tonight." Father says: "Shush. The boy's asleep with a fever."

Ali Safa pulls the desk chair over in front of the bed. Father sits in front of him on the bed letting his legs hang down. Ali Safa sets his glasses in the corner of the room. He shakes his head in amazement. He starts to say something, but then remains quiet.

After a while, he says: "Have you heard about the king's

latest scandal? He had the hots for an officer's wife. He told his commanding officer to assign him to barracks duty. The officer smelled a rat, so he snuck out and went back home and found his wife in bed with the king. The king raised his pistol and blew him away. The next day, he granted the victim's father the status of Pasha. Who knows how much longer the people will put up with this?" Father says: "And what exactly are the people supposed to do? Leave it to God." Ali Safa asks himself: "I wonder who the Muslim Brothers are planning to assassinate now that they've done the secretary for the appeals court."

I struggle to stay awake. His voice begins to slip away. He seems to be talking now in a whisper. I listen carefully: ". . . she's sixteen years old. Her father died and she lives with her mother by herself. They were standing on the stairs in front of our building haggling with the woman who sells butter. Her mother played shy and hid behind a doorway. The girl just stood there. She was wearing a nightshirt that showed lots of cleavage. She had put on a thin line of lipstick. That was the first time I realized that she had grown up. I'd always passed her on the stairway without even noticing her. When she bent over to get the basket of butter, I saw her tits. Pray on the prophet! I pretended I was thinking of buying some. I asked how much it cost. She gave me this shy smile, and I noticed that she was rubbing her lips together, maybe thinking it would make them redder."

Father lights his cigarette and comments: "Girls grow up fast." Ali Safa goes on: "After a few days, I heard her crying out in pain. I knocked on their door. She was limping as she

85

opened for me and she said: 'It's my knee, uncle.'" Father broke in, laughing: "'It's my knee, uncle.'"

Ali Safa continues: "'What's wrong with your knee, sweetheart?' She says that she hit it accidentally. I asked: 'Are you alone?' She answers: 'Mama left.' So I said: 'Show me. Where exactly?' She rested her leg on a chair and pulled up her nightshirt all the way to her knee. Magnificent grace of the Almighty! Don't talk to me about alabaster. Plump and round and shaped like a sculpture! I wanted to bend over and put my lips on it right then and there. I told her: 'Massage it and it'll get better ... or come to think of it, you could rub it with a balm.' I left her standing with her leg on the chair and I went back in to get some of the balm for rheumatism that I rub on my joints. I gave her the tube and told her to rub it on. I was hoping she'd ask me to rub it for her, but instead she put her leg down, took the tube from me, and said: 'Thanks, uncle.'"

As soon as I feel father suddenly turning towards me, I close my eyes. I prick up my ears: "A week later, I was riding the tram. I saw her heading home from school. The tram was crowded. She came close to me, and I stopped her right in front of me. I got a raging hard-on." Father comments: "What luck!" Ali Safa says: "She has to have felt it."

I cough once and then sink into a coughing fit. Father helps me sit up. He leaves the room for a second then comes back with a cup of water. I take a drink. He brings over the bottle of Belmonks with a small spoon. He fills it and brings it close to my mouth. I take a sip grudgingly. He tells me to wait a minute before I lie down again.

Ali Safa says: "Have you heard the latest Dr. Ibrahim Nagy

story? He was walking down the street. He saw a high-class man. He thought it was one of his old patients. He said to him: 'Hello. What's with the long absence? You haven't come around for a while, Muhammad Bey. Your health seems much better, praise God. But you look a bit different. You're fatter and you have a tan now.' The man said: 'But I'm not Muhammad Bey.' Ibrahim Nagy comes right back at him: 'My God! You mean you even changed your name, Muhammad Bey?'"

I lie down and father pulls the covers around me. I turn over and lie on my left side. I close my eyes pretending to sleep. I open them after a minute. Father raises up his legs and sits cross-legged on the bed.

Ali Safa starts telling the story of the Deir Yassin massacre in Palestine. The Zionist forces came in driving an armored car with a loudspeaker on its roof and demanded that the residents come out of their houses if they wanted to save themselves. Some of them believed what was said. They came out of their houses and were mowed down by machine-guns. After that, they threw bombs into the houses where there were women, children, and old people hiding and they killed them all, to the last one.

He got up, shuffled his feet, and said: "It's stuffy. Let's open the balcony doors." Father says: "I'm afraid of the cool breeze on the boy."

Ali Safa sits down and starts talking again in a low voice: "Ever since that day on the tram I can't get her out of my mind. I imagine that she's by herself and knocks on my door at night. She says that she's afraid. She's heard the sound of a burglar... or she has seen a mouse... whatever. I invite her to spend the night at our place with my daughters. I make them a bed on the floor, and I sleep next to them to reassure them. She falls asleep. Maybe she throws an arm across me like she's used to doing with her mother. She turns over and lies with her back to me. If it's hot, she throws off the cover, and if it's cold, even better. I turn over and press my chest to her back. She clings to me, and I'm as hard as iron. She starts to move and I move behind her. My heart pounds. Could she be awake? Could she be sensing what's going on? She must! Maybe she imagines she's dreaming. Her knickers are wet and she's panting. She falls asleep. All of this is in my daydream, of course."

He falls silent. His voice rises again after a second: "I can't get her out of my mind. I thought about asking for her hand from her mother. What do you think, Oh wise one?"

"What would your daughters say?"

"What business is it of theirs? Soon, they'll marry and leave me all alone."

"Are you going to have more kids?"

"Look who's talking?"

Father turns to me and I close my eyes. He says: "The first time I wasn't paying attention."

"What about the second time?"

"The condom broke."

Ali Safa laughs in a loud voice. He stops all of a sudden. He says: "God rest her soul." I turn over on to my back. Father says to him: "Her death left a huge mark on Rowhaya."

"How old was she when you married her?"

"Rowhaya? She was sixteen too."

Ali Safa says in a triumphant tone: "See?"

88

I open my eyes as wide as I can. Father answers in a muffled voice: "I loved her." *The lamp of the living room shines over the table top. It's messier than usual. Smell of sautéed liver. Olives. Pistachios. A small bottle with a clear liquid. Her voice comes from the bedroom. She's singing the Ismahan song over and over: "When will you know it's true? That I love only you." Laughter. Her voice again to a different beat: "Darling, don't let me be. See what's happening to me." My father's voice finishes the song: "Loving you is destroying me!"*

"How did you meet her?"

Father is quiet. I hear him light his cigarette.

"The doctor brought her back when Um Nabila—God rest her soul—was bedridden. She was working for him at the clinic, cleaning and checking in patients. She had a primary school degree. She had the rosiest cheeks. Her father owned a workshop. He had taken a second wife behind her mother's back. The mother was harsh and critical and never gave her a break. She was always beating her ... Nabila and her brother had married and left the house. I suddenly found someone to talk to. She read the papers and even talked to me about politics. She paid attention to all kinds of things. I remember her telling me that Hitler would end in disaster and that Gandhi was going to be killed. She engaged my mind. It was the first time in my life that I fell in love. Can you imagine that? A fifty-five year old man falls in love. I said let's get married and she agreed. Her father complained about the difference in age. She told him: 'So what? I love him.' I married her in secret."

I listened like I was under a magic spell. Father kept talking: "I rented an apartment nearby, the one you know in front of the Jewish school. I followed God's will in the whole thing. I'd sleep every night next to Um Nabila. In the morning, I'd go to the office. At the end of the day, I'd run to the second apartment." *He appears at the door of the apartment in his white three-piece suit with fez. He has a white umbrella in his right hand. A paper bag full of fruit rests on his left arm. His dark face is beaming. He bends over me and wraps his arms around me.*

"As soon as night broke, I'd get dressed to go back to the old house. She hung on to me. She pleaded with me to stay until bedtime. She would say that she was afraid to be left alone. She closed all the shutters and lit up the lights of the apartment. She shrunk herself up in bed. She would lie down and read the Quran until she dozed off. She would wake up scared in the middle of the night. She would hear soft voices calling to her, so she'd cling hard to the bed and plug up her ears until the sun came up."

I notice a bedbug coming toward my head. I don't want to move, so father won't see that I'm awake. I know it's going to bite me once the lights are out and keep me from sleeping. I follow it with my eyes to see where it will hide.

"Finally, Um Nabila died. We had done with all the mourning, and Nabila says: 'Come on, Papa, stay with me.' I told her I was married and had a second house. She was angry and her brother went crazy and told me: 'Now you're going to mate like rabbits and have lots of little ones, aren't you?' But I went ahead and settled in the new house, and I had a taste of what it was like to be happy."

He was quiet. He lit a cigarette again. "When I had Nabila and her brother, I was still a young man and I spent most of my time outside the house. This time I really enjoyed being a father. Especially after I retired." He turned towards me and I closed my eyes. "I'll never forget the sight of him coming into the room, opening up the drawers, and rifling through the books. Whenever he saw something new, he would point to it and say: 'That?' Then it became: 'What's that?' He would try to show me that he understood. I won't forget the sight of him the first time he ever stood up. He wobbled two steps toward me and clapped. He felt he had achieved something great."

I drift off then wake up to the buzzing of a mosquito next to my ear. I call upon God to keep it from biting me. The voice of Ali Safa: "I'll go crazy. At night I toss and turn, wanting a soft body in my embrace. We wouldn't even have to do anything."

Father says: "So what are you going to do, my friend? Your only option is to stare."

"You said it. When I was coming over I saw a girl running in the street. Her tits were bouncing around. I thought I could hear the sound of her buttocks bouncing against each other. Now everything reminds me of what used to be. A shawl wrapped snugly around a tight ass. Two lips slipping through the covering of a burka. A plump arm in short sleeves or a bare shoulder under a sleeveless blouse."

Quiet settles over them both. The radio plays in the constable's room. Fareed al-Atrash. I notice the bedbug scooting across the wall. It wants to get away from the light. I reach out my finger and crush it, then I hold my breath, so I won't have to smell its stink.

Father's voice: "It was the first month that I went to get my pension. There was an old man wearing a checkered coat, a dark-colored shirt, and a tattered necktie. The edge of his fez had a sweat stain. He was leaning on a cane. He wore Coke-bottle glasses. You had no idea where he was looking. When his turn came, he didn't move. He kept standing quietly as though he was daydreaming and he was ready to just wait there until the next day. The clerk at the cashier's window knew me. He made my payments. He stretched out his hand to get my claim certificate. I got up and waved at the old man to go ahead of me. He said something I couldn't hear. The clerk motioned him over to the next window. He started to move with a great effort, so I helped him make it to the next window. Not only did he not thank me, he didn't even look at me. It was like I wasn't there. When I went out, I saw him standing there, leaning against a lamp post. He kept standing there for a long time, looking straight ahead. It was like he had forgotten where he was. I couldn't go near him. Give me another two or three years and I'll be just like him."

Ali Safa says: "Don't even think that way, friend. It's still too soon for that." I feel father shaking his head. "I've started to trip when I'm walking along. My eyes glaze over. I don't hear well. My molars hurt, but when I go to the dentist, he says my gums are shrinking." Safa says: "The important thing is your virility." Father's voice comes to me as though he is far away: "What virility? It's just a couple of drops now. The old power hose isn't there anymore."

a picture of Tarzan on it. The salesman scolds me and grabs it out of my hands. I buy a notebook of songs for five millimes then keep walking. Stumping my foot in the dirt, I notice a round piece of iron. I back away from it. I make a point of going around the shop of the sheikh of the quarter. Finally, I come to the house. I ring the bell but father doesn't answer. I ring again and Mrs. Tahiya opens up. She says: "Your father's gone out. Close the door behind you." She leaves me alone and heads for the kitchen. I close the door to the apartment. I push on the door to our room and find it's locked. I have the key. I go in and put my satchel on the desk. Take off my clothes and put on the pyjamas with the shiny buttons. I go back to the door. Stand at the threshold listening. I come out into the living area.

The sound of the primus stove is coming from the kitchen. I take light steps out toward the hallway. I avoid looking in the direction of the toilet. I come close to the door of the kitchen. Cling to the wall. My head leans out with care. She's sitting on the little kitchen stool and peeling cloves of garlic. There's a plate of *ful* beans next to her. I take a step back towards the living room. I go around the table to the door to her room. It's open. I go closer. On top of the bed, there's a blue patterned dress and on the floor are white shoes with high heels. On the wall a big picture hangs in a gilded frame. In it, the constable wears a military uniform. He's smiling. He has a high fez on and it is leaning to the left. A chiffonier to the right has a big mirror over it in a pale-colored metal frame. The mirror is sitting on the top of the chiffonier. It has a crack at the top of the glass. On top of the chiffonier many things are scattered including a box of chocolates. Would she notice if I took one?

I prick up my ears. She's singing in the kitchen: "the day we met, we two . . ." Her voice comes closer.

I back away from the door to the room. Stop next to the door to the skylight. I can look down into the window of Um Zakiya. It is closed and darkened. She comes into the living room. A cup of tea is in her hand. She heads towards her room, and waves at me to follow her. She sets the cup down on top of the chiffonier. She opens the box of chocolates and takes out a piece wrapped in shiny gold foil. She hands it to me. She asks about my mother. My face goes red. I don't answer. *She's sitting in a chair in the middle of the living room and her thick hair is hanging down over her shoulders. She's crying: "Ahhh! My head!" Her face looks like she is in pain. My father gives her a piece of ice. She puts it on her head and presses it.*

She lights a cigarette. She leans over the mirror set against the wall. She combs her hair and studies her features. She twists her hair in a bun on the side. Her finger spreads a bit of lipstick over her full lips. It's the first time I have seen a woman putting on make-up because mother never used it. *Her lower lip is cracked, with drops of blood trickling from it.*

I am under a spell watching her. With each movement, her face becomes more beautiful. My eyes meet hers in the mirror. I turn red. I suddenly come forward, saying: "Mama Tahiya, you're very pretty." She takes me in her arms and pulls me to her chest. Her clean smell with hints of Lux soap creeps up my nose. She covers my face with kisses, planting them on my eyes, cheeks, and mouth, saying: "You're pretty too." She pulls me back from her chest and studies me. She stretches out her finger towards my mouth and pulls apart my lips, then she tugs on the lower one lightly as though she's tickling a small child. A serious smile flickers in her eyes. She pulls me in again. She says in a hushed voice: "I have a son who's two years younger than you." I ask her: "Where is he?" She says: "With his father." Tears start welling up in her eyes. All of a sudden, her features brighten and she laughs.

She pulls me away from her and points to my cheeks and lips: "Your face is covered in red. Look." I come close to the chiffonier and look up into the mirror. She leads me next to her and sits down on the edge of the bed. She brings me between her legs, takes a wet towel and wipes off my face for me. She runs her fingers through my hair. She starts to pick through it while she sings. I kiss her on her soft arms and shoulders. I ask her to tell me a story.

She thinks for a second, then starts: "There was an old man who was very poor and had a son." I look at her, suspicious. She keeps going: "They were living in an apartment on the second floor." I know now that she means father and me. I am mad because she called us poor. I decide to complain to father when I leave. I step back away from her. She hugs me as she laughs: "Don't be angry." I step out of her hold, all mad. She gives me a pat and tries to make up. She says: "Come on. Let's go out." I say: "What about papa?"

"He's not coming until late. Get dressed, so we can go."

I go to our room. After a while, she calls to me. I tell her I'm putting on clothes to go out in. She says: "You don't have to. You can just come in your pyjamas."

"What about shoes?"

"Just come in your house slippers." I go to her room and

find she has put on the blue patterned dress and white shoes. She wraps a black shawl around herself. She smooths its edge over her head to cover her hair and wraps it tightly around her waist. She studies herself in the mirror, spinning around to see her back. I suggest that she writes a note to father to tell him that we went out. She says: "You write it. I don't know how." *Mother sharpens the pencil. The tip breaks. She gives it to my father along with the sharpener. He puts the sharpener down, brings a razor, and whittles down the pencil with care. He never lets the tip break. She turns to a clean page in her big notebook.*

I write out the note and put it on top of our bed. I lock the door to our room and put the key in my pocket. We walk out of the building, turn left, and head up the street. The snack shop and the clothes presser's shop. Heads turn to us. Eyes follow us. One of the men sitting in front of the dried fish shop yells out: "O Pasha!" I know that he's calling out to us. I look at the ground. She keeps walking, sure of herself and carefree. Bags of cotton are set out in front of the upholstery shop. It's brushed and made into rolls set in the middle of the shop. *He sits in the living room. He beats the rug with a strap fixed to a large stick. Mother opens the window on to the courtyard to let the dust out of the house. He straightens out the sheet covers. I hide the scissors from him. He becomes crazy looking for them.*

We cross the wide street and pass in front of the church then turn towards a dark alley. There's another alley at the end. A cart is set up in front of it carrying a barrel of pickles. A dark and dirty entrance. We go up some narrow stairs. A rotting smell. I stumble on one of the steps. She catches me with her hand and brings me to her. We stop in front of the door to an apartment. She knocks. A little girl opens the door, carrying an oil lamp. She leads us into a living room with no furniture. It opens on to a room with a wide bed in it. A woman is lying on it under the covers. She could be the same age as Mama Tahiya, or a little older. There's a handkerchief around her neck. Mama Tahiya says: "What's wrong with you, Sabah?" She answers in a hoarse voice: "Just a touch of cold." She looks at me smiling.

"His son?"

Mama Tahiya starts laughing: "No. He's *my* son."

"You're kidding."

"He's the neighbor's son."

She pulls off the cover and throws it on a chair. Sabah studies her dress. Mama Tahiya asks: "What is it? Do you like it or something?"

"A lot."

"He's the one who bought it for me."

She sits on the edge of the bed and I sit next to her. She grabs a picture magazine off the top of the covers. She opens it up to the fashion page and points to a silk dress with a flower pattern and ruffles covering it from top to bottom. Next to it there's a handbag made from wicker. She says: "I'd like a dress like this." Mama Tahiya answers: "It's divine!" Sabah puts the magazine down and asks about the constable. Mama Tahiya says: "They transferred him to the south."

"Why?"

"Because the police went on strike."

"So why did they go on strike?"

"They want to make the same money and get the same promotions as the army."

Sabah says: "The nurses are on strike too. They're only making four or five pounds. What are they supposed to do with that?"

"Don't they get tips too from the patients?" Sabah says that her brother-in-law got knocked on the head when the police raided the Qasr al-Aini Hospital.

"So what came of it?"

"What came of what? They just fired something like a thousand nurses and put new ones in their place."

The covers slip down and she gets out of the bed. She is wearing a flannel *gallabiya* with long sleeves. The white background is patterned with tiny flowers. She leans over a primus stove near the wall. After lighting it, she sets down a small brass kettle for making Turkish coffee. She looks at me: "Shall I order a cool drink for you?"

Mama Tahiya says: "No, we're leaving right away." She gives me a sweet. Mama Tahiya says: "I heard they're planning on closing the houses. They're saying they're a violation of religious law."

"And they just figured that out?"

"What are you going to do?"

Sabah says: "The doing is all up to the Lord. He doesn't forget his servants." She pours the coffee into two glasses. They sip at it without talking. Sabah lights a Hollywood brand cigarette. She gives one to Mama Tahiya. She asks her: "Is he planning on marrying you?"

Mama Tahiya answers while inhaling her cigarette: "Don't know."

I make it to the square then head off to the right. I cross both Qamr and Ahmad Said streets. Follow along the tram line down al-Zahir street to about half way. Cross the street running right in front of a Jewish snack stand. I spend two millimes on a tube of roasted white melon seeds. They're smaller than the large brown seeds but they're cracked and have their own special taste. I put the tube in the pocket of my pyjamas.

I go back towards the square then stop in front of the tobacconist on the corner. I buy a pack of cigarettes for father. The salesman gives me a green pack instead of the yellow one I asked for. I go back home, tripping over a water jar in my path. Mud covers my twisted sandals made from tire rubber. I wipe them across the steps to the front door trying to get rid of it. I turn the key in the door to the apartment. The lamp in the living room still lights up the room as when I left. The door to the constable's room is closed. The sound of the radio comes floating out from behind it. The door to our room is also closed. I put the pack of cigarettes on top of the sideboard. I come up to the wash basin. I take off the sandals and wash them.

I pick up the pack of cigarettes and head into our room. Father is sitting cross-legged on top of the bed. His eyes are red and he is frowning. He's always this way after he wakes up from an afternoon nap. I hand him the pack of cigarettes. He blows up in anger: "Didn't I tell you 'Tuscany'? Now you've gone and brought me Tuscanilly." I say the salesman gave me that pack. "Don't you have a tongue to tell him what you want? You're totally useless all the way around." I offer to go back to the shop and exchange the pack. He cools off a bit and says: "That's okay. Maybe he doesn't have the right ones. Make me a cup of coffee."

I go out to the living area. Stand in front of the sideboard. Take down the small brass coffee kettle. I put a spoon of coffee and another of sugar in to the kettle. I pour in the water from the jug and take up a spoon to stir it all together. There's an alcohol stove sitting at my eye level. I take off the brass cover and strike a match to light the flame. I set the tiny coffee kettle on it. Mama Tahiya's door is still closed and the sounds of the radio still echo behind it.

I step over toward the door to the skylight. Um Zakiya's window is shut. I hurry back to the coffee and wait there patiently until it starts to bubble up. I pull away the kettle before it boils over. I put it back over the flame a few more times then put the brass cover back on to put out the flame. Carefully, I pour the coffee from the kettle into a cup then pick it up and take it to our room. I'm walking slowly to make sure not to shake the cup so much that the coffee loses its frothy head. He takes the cup from me and I bring him the jar of water. He takes a loud slurp from it. *Mother raises the jar up in the air and*

*pours water into her mouth without her lips touching the edge. I try to
do the same and get my clothes all wet.*

He lights a cigarette. I sit at my desk. Pour some seeds
from the tube out in front of me. I open the English reader.
He finishes drinking his coffee, gets off the bed, and throws a
towel over his shoulder. He lights a lamp and heads towards
the bathroom to wash for prayer. When he comes back in, he
stretches out the prayer rug on the floor. He prays the sundown prayer. He pulls open the glass doors to the balcony, and
pushes out the wooden shutters to open them too. He drags
the desk chair over to the narrow balcony, sits down, and lays
his right arm on its metal railing. I stand next to him. *Mother
comes in with a cup of coffee singing: "I am in love and I bring you your
coffee." My father slurps the coffee loudly. He lights his black cigarette.
He sits next to the open window. He leaves his cigarette sitting on the
ashtray. Gets up to pray the sundown prayer. He comes back to relight
his cigarette. A gas worker appears at the top of the street. He leans his
ladder against a lamp post, climbs up, pulls open the glass pane of the
lamp, relights it, closes the glass pane again, and comes down. He puts
the ladder on his shoulder. He moves to the next lamppost.*

The balcony across from us is closed and dark. The window
next to it is opened and lit up. We know it is a guest room
that is only opened when they have visitors. Its curtains are
rippling. There is a pale light in the apartment on the second
floor where the iron merchant lives with his two wives. The
light is in the first wife's room. It's put out and then comes
on in the room of the second wife. The voice of Um Safwat
screams at her son. Our Coptic neighbor Abu Wadie, appears
coming out from the entrance to the alley. He wears a dark

suit. He carries sacks under his arms. He stops in front of the door to our house, and calls just like every night: "Wadie!" He exchanges good evenings with father. His wife answers him from the apartment above ours. Just like every night, he says to her: "The basket." She lowers it down to him so he can put the sacks in it. The basket goes up slowly. He comes in to the house.

Father leans his head over so he can see Sabry Effendi. His oldest daughter Siham has on a sleeveless nightshirt. She's leaning over with her chest against the edge of the window. Behind her, her sisters are making a commotion. Her eyes are fixed on the entrance to the alley. She pulls back inside when the young man who lives in the room on the roof appears. He's a handsome engineering student. His skin is white, like the foreigners, and he wears glasses with gilded frames.

Father draws back his head. He watches the window next to the balcony across from ours. The breeze is wafting through its curtains. There's a chair with a high back and a man in a dark-colored suit is sitting in it. There's a low table in front of him with little black things in rows arranged on top of it. He turns them in his hand and then puts them back carefully.

He says: "I wonder if that's the groom?" We know that Hikmet is supposed to be having an engagement party today. Father tells me to turn off the light. We sit in the dark with our eyes fixed on the window across from us. Abu Zakiya comes up from the direction of the entrance to the alley. He's thin and dark with grey hair. One of his eyes is closed all the way. He walks slowly, as though he is tired out. He's so quiet by nature that you hardly hear his voice. He does not notice us before he goes into the building next door. Father says: "How strange that they found each other." He means his wife, who is white and much younger.

He stretches out his head and focuses on something: "What are those things over there?" I try to follow his gaze. Are they glasses of sherbet punch? No one's going near them. In fact, there's no sign of anyone else around, as if no one is in the room but the man in the chair. No one is ululating and there are no sounds of a party. Father says: "It could be little lumps of hashish for a hookah." After a while he adds: "That's weird. Look harder."

I balance my glasses again and take a harder look, but I can't make out the black things. Father suggests that I wipe the lenses of my glasses. I go back into the room and wipe them with the bed sheet. I go back to the balcony. The man is still sitting looking at the little things in front of him. Father stretches his arm out to me without turning toward me. He whispers: "Loan me your glasses." I take them off and hand them to him. He brings them close to his face without putting them on. He shakes his head, then he hands back the glasses, saying: "It's no use."

He prays the afternoon prayer. He sits me down in front of him on the bed. He rests his glasses on the end of his nose and, from the geography book, begins to explain to me the difference between straits, a gulf and an isthmus. He scolds me for forgetting. He's annoyed. Gives me memorization exercises. He dresses and goes out. I hear him ask Mama Tahiya if she will look after me and say that he'll probably be out until late.

I listen to his steps falling on the stairs and wait to see him come out into the lane, then I leave our room. Mama Tahiya is hanging her laundry out on the clothes line strung between the entrance to the living room and the door to her room. She has brought out a bucket of water and is cleaning the room and washing down their door with soap. I bring her jugs of water from the sink. She wipes down the floor of the living room while singing, "I'll meet him tomorrow and the day after . . ." She brings in the primus stove from the kitchen along with the small wooden foot stool that sits just inches off the ground. She puts them both in the middle of the guest room next to the washbasin made of zinc. She brings in half a cup of sugar from her room. She adds half a cup of water to it and stirs them for a long time, then pours the mixture into a small metal pan. She puts it on the fire, pulls the end of her dress up between her legs, and sits down on the stool. Fading sunlight comes in from the window to the skylight. It falls across her bare knees.

I come in and sit on the couch. The sugar and water start to boil. She squeezes a lemon into it and stirs it some more. I ask her what she's doing. She says: "Halva for the hair." *Um Ibrahim gives me a small piece, then carries the pan to my mother in the bathroom. She closes the door behind her.*

She goes on stirring until the mixture becomes a soft transparent paste. She lifts the pan off the flame and puts it down on the floor. I follow her as she leaves the room. She fills a tin pan with water, brings it back in, and puts it on the fire. She touches the paste to see how hot it is. She gives me a tidbit. I put it in my mouth and suck on it. She spreads out the paste, kneads it with her hands, and keeps on working it until the paste gets softer and turns a dark color. She rolls out the paste, cuts off a small section, and spreads it tightly over her forearm, then yanks it off all at once. She presses it a little more with her fingers to keep it soft. She does the same thing again and again until she gets down to her hand, then she throws that piece away and takes up another piece. She raises her arm up high and flattens the piece on her armpit. She pulls it off quickly. She keeps doing it until her underarm is soft and white, then she moves to her other arm.

The front doorbell rings. I stand behind the door and yell out: "Who's there?" A woman's voice answers: "I am Attiyat.

Is Tahiya there?" I run back to the room to tell Mama Tahiya who it is. She tells me: "Let her in. She's my cousin."

I open the door. Dark and tall and wrapped tightly in a shawl. She follows me into the living room and slaps her chest, saying: "Oh no! Not in front of the boy!" Mama Tahiya answers back without a care as she passes her hand lightly over her bare arm: "What's the big deal?" She sits down and asks when the constable will get home. Mama Tahiya says: "Maybe tomorrow. Send the kids to spend the night with me tonight. Have Ragui bring his tar drum with him." Attiyat stands up and wraps her shawl tightly around her. She passes a look from Mama Tahiya to me and then goes out.

Mama Tahiya moves on to her other armpit. She twists her head to have a good look at it. She touches it with her finger. Stands up. She takes me gently by my ear and says: "Off to your room. Sit in there and don't come out." I take her hand and plead with her: "Please no, mama, by the prophet, don't leave me there alone." She studies me with a smile: "Okay. You can sit in the living room on one condition: don't look in on me." She turns on the light. I bring my geography book and sit down at the table by the front door.

I put the book in front of me, opening it to the notebook full of songs stuck between its pages. She moves quickly back and forth between her room and the living room, carrying clothes over her arm. She has Lux soap, a loofah, and a small mirror in her hand. She goes to the sink to fill a tin pan with water then carries it to the living room. She comes back to the door to her room and closes it. She shakes her finger at me and warns: "Don't get up from your place until I'm done."

"What if someone knocks?"

As she goes through the living room, she says: "Don't answer."

"Well, what if Tante Attiyat comes back?"

She closes the door behind her saying: "Don't worry. She's not coming."

"What about papa?"

"He has a key."

"Or if the lights go out?"

"When that happens, I'll tell you what to do."

I open the song book. I look for the song, "I am in love and I bring you your coffee." I put the songbook aside. Stand up carefully. I sneak away from my place without letting the chair move. The electric light grows dim until it almost disappears, then comes back weakly.

I turn the knob on her door. I push on the door and go in. The light is on. I go towards the chiffonier. A photograph is pressed between the corner of the metal frame and the surface of the mirror. She is next to the constable in a crowded street. She wears a sleeveless dress and high heels, and he is wearing a dress shirt and slacks. The top of the chiffonier is cluttered with many things: a Gazelle brand bottle of perfume, tacks, a sewing needle, a spool of thread, a broken eyeliner pencil, an old thimble, a tube of lipstick in a brass case, a can of yellowish face powder, hairpins, torn playing cards, an old picture of her with a piece torn off and the torn piece showing a part of a leg in a man's shoe, a small pack of Hollywood brand cigarettes (the kind that holds five of them), a silver strip of aspirin tablets, a dried up key lime, a toothbrush, a bottle of Anatolian hair oil, a steel comb, a metal statuette of a naked woman and a metal ashtray with a slanted edge.

I pull on one of its drawers. Pieces of clothing are carefully arranged. I push it back the way it was and pull on the one above it. A jar of jam. A box of pieces of cheese shaped like triangles. A large metal cigarette case. I close the drawer. Leave the room. I gently pull the door shut behind me.

I lightly move over to the door to the guest room. I press my eye against the keyhole. I see her sitting on the kitchen stool. Her right side is turned to me, so I can't see her face. She is leaning over her folded right leg. A piece of halva sits on top of her foot. She pulls it up and smoothens it, then she puts it on the middle of her leg. She repeats the move higher up on her thigh. She turns toward the door and I jump back quickly. I hurry over to my seat. I sit down and open the song book, flipping through the pages. I linger over the songs of Ismahan. I listen. The sound of the stove.

I leave my seat again and step carefully toward the door. I look through the keyhole. Her back is to me. She takes up a piece of halva and puts it between her legs, then yanks it off. She lets out an "Ouch!" She takes the last piece; she puts it between her legs. She pulls it with force. She does the same thing over again a few times. She's panting. She picks up a piece of rock, about the size of a Jaffa orange. She rubs it against her heels and turns towards the stove. The steam rises up from the pan. She uses a jar to pour warm water into the zinc basin. She stands up and stretches her hands out to pull off her *gallabiya*. Steam fills up the lenses of my glasses. I take them off and wipe them on my pyjamas. *Mama Basima is naked on top of the*

toilet. Her hair is colored with henna. I stand between her huge legs. She
pours water over my body as she studies my little prick.

The sound of steps echoes in the stairwell. I hurry to my seat and open my geography book. The two feet stop in front of our door. They continue on up the stairs. I am about to get up again when I hear the sound of the stove being turned off and I stay frozen in my seat.

The guest room door opens. Mama Tahiya comes out. She is wearing a nightshirt held up by shoulder straps. Her hair is wrapped in a big towel. She asks me: "Are you done?" I shake my head. I take the geography textbook and the notebook of songs and I follow her into her room.

She pulls the chair over and sits down. She takes off her clogs and lifts her feet up on to the edge of the bed. She looks at her heels. They glow red. Her two legs are shiny in the room's light. She puts her feet down and stands, turning in the direction of the mirror. She unwraps the towel, picks up a comb and raises her arm up to her head. Her smooth underarm is shiny. As she combs her long hair, the water comes dripping off it. I sit on the bed. She leans in front of the mirror, pulling her hair out in front of my eyes. She lets it hang down in even strands on either side of her face. I tell her: "Put it in a bun." She gathers her hair and makes a ball out of it on top of her head. She puts lipstick on her finger and colors her lips with it. She turns to me: "Am I pretty?" My face turns red.

The front doorbell rings and I run to answer it. It's two boys my age. One of them has smooth hair that he has parted on the side. The other is very dark skinned and carries a small drum underneath his arm. I lead them to the room. We leave our slippers at the door. The three of us sit on the edge of the bed. The two boys ignore me. She gives each of us a piece of Nestle cheese, a cookie and a piece of chocolate.

I hear father's voice calling me. I leave the songbook on the bed and pick up my geography textbook. I go out to the living room. He stands at the door to our room holding his fez in his hand. He leads me inside then asks me if I've studied. I swear to him that I have. He takes me to the toilet to pee then tells me to get ready for bed. I beg him to let me stay up and play in Mama Tahiya's room. He says it's late. I answer: "Tomorrow's Friday."

"What about dinner?"

"I already ate."

He gives in. I run to her. She's wearing her white robe. She tells me: "Ask your father if he wants to have tea?" She leaves the room and heads toward the kitchen. I scamper to him and ask from behind the door. He answers, "No." I call to her from the hallway: "No, he doesn't want any." I head back to her room. The boy with the parted hair is in front of the chiffonier. He puts some lipstick on his fingers then brushes his lips and takes a look at his face in the mirror. Mama Tahiya brings the tea. She bursts out laughing at the sight of him and says: "Holy hell, Effat, you little devil. You've turned yourself into a pretty little girl like the moon." We sit on the floor. She pours tea into small cups for us. She takes a tambourine with little brass ringlets around its edges out from under the bed. When she shakes it, the ringlets jingle. She hands it to the boy.

She starts singing along with Abdel Wahab: "Our night is like wine, yearning croons like a dove. O my darling, this is the night of our love." The other boy starts to beat the tambourine.

He says to her: "Dance for us, *ubla.*" She takes off her robe and ties a white towel around her waist. She sings: "You, You, No one but you . . ." Her body moves to the beat of the tambourine and drum. She's all caught up in watching her breasts bounce lightly. She stretches her arm in front of her. Her palms clasp each other. She snaps her fingers. Gets up on her tiptoes. She shakes her middle in short trembles that follow one after the other. She shoots a smile at me. Blood rushes to my face.

As she finishes dancing, she is panting from the effort. She pulls two blankets from on top of the bed. She unfolds them and spreads them out on the floor. We sit down on them cross legged. She pulls out the playing cards. We play a round of battle. Then she suggests that we play Old Maid. She takes out three of the kings and shuffles the cards. She says: "Whoever is left with the last king has to do what we say."

She deals. I draw a card. Seven of Hearts. I have another seven. I put them together and set them on the floor. The other two play quickly and with skill. We look up at each others' faces. We're trying to figure out who has it. I draw another card and it comes up the king. All the cards in our hands seem to empty out quickly. We put them down on the floor. I'm left with the king. *We draw the hopscotch boxes on the pavement with chalk. Six wide boxes with a half circle at the top. I stand on one leg. I toss the pebble across the line. I manage to move from box to box. My father watches me from the window. I make it to the half circle and name myself the champion.*

She says: "What shall we make you do?"

Effat says: "He should get down on his hands and knees and go around us in a circle barking."

She looks at me, hesitates, then says: "No. He should sing to us."

I say: "I can't sing."

"So what? Sing 'The Postman Complains From All My Letters.'"

I recite the song without being able to get its tune right.

We start to play again. My eyelids feel heavy.

I am having a hard time fighting off sleep. She says: "That's enough." She looks at me: "Ask permission from your father to spend the night with us." I find him sitting on the bed resting his back against the headboard. He is reading a book. I beg him to let me spend the night with them. He says okay. I go back to the room.

She goes with us to the bathroom and stands waiting in the entrance to the hallway while we go. The boys wash their feet in the sink. We go back to the room. She unfolds the two blankets and lays them out on the floor. She waves at the two boys to lie down on them and gives them a long pillow. She covers them with a blanket. She says to me: "Sleep next to the wall so you don't fall off the bed."

I put my glasses on the chiffonier. Lie down on the bed. I stretch out beside the wall. She takes off her robe. The light goes out. She lies down next to me. She pulls me to her chest. My head snuggles against her breasts. I can smell her clean scent. She moves away and turns her back to me. She says: "Sweet dreams, my boys." The two boys answer in unison: "Sweet dreams, *ubla*." I say, "Sweet dreams, mama." She spreads a blanket over us. I fall asleep. Suddenly, I am awake again. I can't move. I realize I'm in her grasp and my leg is between her thighs. I hear her panting. She pulls me tight. I say to her: "Mama, do you want something?" She doesn't answer. I move my leg out from between her thighs but she hangs on to me. She moves away a moment later. Her snoring rises up over us.

The dark face with its two red eyes comes slowly closer from behind the metal grating that lines the window. I recognize Abbas. The door opens and an oil lamp with long rectangular panes of fine glass appears. The lamp comes closer. Its flame grows. The white round face of Mama Tahiya comes into view behind it. Her hair is up. Her lips are covered with lipstick. The constable is behind her. He tries to hold her, but she resists. She pounds her fists against his chest with all her might trying to get out of his grasp. She screams: "That's your son ... Your son, you liar, you cheat!" I'm surprised that she doesn't recognize me. I open my mouth to start to tell her who I am, but my mother's face suddenly appears in place of hers. Blood flows out of the cut on her lower lip. Her face shrinks and then twists up. It disappears. Two big hairy arms appear in its place. They come at me. I want to scream, but the sound can't make it out of my mouth.

I wake up suddenly and I shudder. The light is shining. I call for father. I sit up. Sweat drips off me. I push away the covers and slide over to the edge of the bed. Tears sprout up in my eyes. I jump down and push on the door of the room until it opens. The light is on in the hallway. I call out again: "Papa?" "Mama Tahiya?" No one answers. The constable's room is shut.

I take a side glance over towards the toilet. I open the door to the apartment. My eyes move to the darkened landing. I shoot a glance at the corner, where the storage room is. I leave the door open and run down the steps to the entrance. I keep running out into the alley all the way to the main street. I turn right and keep running all the way to the shop of sheikh of the quarter.

Even without my glasses, I know the men seated on the chairs on the sidewalk in front. They are Sheikh Abdel 'Alim, Refaat Effendi, and the priest. I see father sitting to the side. He's listening carefully to the turbaned sheikh in his glasses. I rush over to him. He turns to me frowning. I stand between his knees. He says to me: "What are you doing here?" A fit of coughing takes hold of me. He feels my throat and chest. "See how sweaty you are?" He stands up and says to the sheikh: "Excuse us, my good sheikh."

He grabs my hand violently and pulls me through the lane all the way to the house. He closes the door of the apartment behind us and pushes me into our room. "Get up. Lie down on the bed." He bends over me and tucks the covers around me. "Can't you stay by yourself for even a little while? Do you think an *afreet* will eat you or something? Do I have to pull you along by the hand every place I go?"

He moves away from me and sits down on the bed. I cough. He goes out to the balcony, moving out of my sight. Then he comes back in and walks towards the door of the apartment. "I'm fed up. That's it. What did I do to deserve this torture? I should've done like Aly Safa. He couldn't give a damn about his daughters." *The chair turns into something like a cart that sells cucumbers and red dates. Its wooden brake keeps me from losing control*

give me some respite." I cough again. I shudder. My teeth start to chatter. I blink my eyes. *The angels are surrounding me. Mother carries me. Light comes in from the hallway. It swirls around me in circles.*

I open my eyes. The light is spinning in circles. His head is bent over me. It is covered with his woolen cap. That means he won't go out again. He feels around my temples. He lifts my head up and puts a spoon of Belmonks in my mouth. He unfolds a wet handkerchief. Spreads it over my forehead. He disappears. He comes back with a glass of water, and squeezes two lemons into it. He brings out the aspirin bottle. He empties two pills into his hand. Dissolves them into the water. He raises my head. Forces me to drink. After the first sip, I push the cup away with my hand. I can't breathe, so I open my mouth to breathe through it. My chest heaves and I gasp for air. He pulls me to his chest. Raises a handkerchief to my nose. He tells me to blow. My nose is clogged. *He raises a small mirror in front of my face. I see my two nostrils stained with bright red spots of mercurochrome.*

He leaves the bed. I follow him with my eyes. He opens the dresser and starts to root around in it. He comes back with a thin glass tube. He gets up on to the bed. Leans over me. Puts the end of the tube in one of my nostrils. He drains the stuff clogging one nostril. He dumps it on a plate. Then he does the other nostril. He drains it and dumps it. I can breathe again. He puts his hand on my head and recites the verse of the throne from the Quran. *The coughing won't stop. I'm parched, and he gives me a drink of a coloring of iodine mixed with water. He takes me to a well that has a gas smell coming up from it. He sits me down at its edge. He tells me to lean my head over and breathe in. The well is deep. His strong arms surround me and hold me back from falling.*

I open the door carefully and look behind me. Father is deep into his nap. I go out to the living room. I walk softly to the door of the constable's room. It is shut. I put my eye to the keyhole. The end of the bed. Four bare feet over it. The feet are all tangled and they're not moving. I go over to the skylight and have a look at the window of Um Zakiya. It is open. The side of her bare arm is showing. I go around the table. I notice a mouse running towards the bathroom and the kitchen. I go back to Mama Tahiya's room. I hear moving inside, so I hurry back to our room.

Father is sleeping on his left side with his back to me. He's snoring. I sit at the desk and open up my science book.

I hear movement in the living room and hurry back to the door to look through the keyhole. The constable has a T-shirt and pyjama bottoms on and is standing in front of the wash basin. He washes up, then goes back to his room. I wait. Mama Tahiya is in her white robe. I wait until she finishes washing and goes back. I open the door and go out to the living room. She waves at me to follow her to the room.

The constable is lying on the bed. He is still in the t-shirt. His hands are clasped behind his head, leaning against the wall. The hair under his arms is thick. The bed covers are piled up. She pulls them off to make a place for me. She gives me a plate with lotus fruit that I love so much and says: "Kareem brought it back with him from Assyut." She combs her hair in front of the mirror then passes the lipstick over her lips.

I pick out a fat orange-colored piece. Wipe it off with the sleeve of my pyjamas. I love the taste of the fruit's dry, sweet flesh. I spit out the seed and look around me, not knowing what to do with it. I end up putting it in my pocket. I pick out another. It's bitter. I spit it out and choose a red one instead.

I look up at Mama Tahiya. She lets her hair down below her shoulders. Her eyes shine. She looks at "Kareem." Some anger shows on his face. She smiles. I feel that he's annoyed at my being there.

"Shall I make tea?"

She leaves the room without waiting for him to answer. I notice a picture magazine tossed to the side of the bed. I grab it and start flipping through its pages. A picture of the king at his meeting with the army officers heading to Palestine. In a military uniform with short sleeves. He holds the end of a staff under his arm. His glasses have big black frames. His thick moustache has two raised ends on either side of his mouth. He has a beret on his head leaning to the right.

I ask the constable: "So, are we going to war?" He says it has to happen now that Israel has declared statehood. He adds: "There's also America; they said they'd cut off petrol and farming materials if we go into Palestine."

Mama Tahiya comes back carrying a tray with three cups of tea. We drink them without talking. She throws herself into gathering up the playing cards scattered all over the room. She organizes them and counts them out while sitting cross-legged. Her robe slides up and shows her bare legs.

She says: "Come on. Let's play Old Maid."

She sets aside three cards with old kings on them. She shuffles the cards again. The constable turns over on to his left side. He leans on his right elbow and draws a card. I look at my cards. I notice his hand sneaking to the thigh of Mama Tahiya. She laughs and pulls her body away. We start to run out of cards quickly. He only has one card left. He lays it down to reveal the other king.

Mama Tahiya claps: "What shall we make you do?" She adds: "Cover your eyes." *My father teaches mother to play poker. He laughs when he wins. She puts the cards on the table and says: "This game is forbidden by God." He says: "Go on, old lady. We're playing for small change." She's stubborn: "No! It's forbidden."*

He lies on his back. She pulls out a sash and kneels on top of it. He stretches his hand toward her chest, but she gets away. She wraps the sash around his eyes and ties it over his ear. She waves to me to come closer, then whispers: "Spit in his mouth." She tells him to open his mouth. He does it. I lean over him. I spit.

He shivers, sits up, and screams: "You dog! You son of a bitch!" He unties the sash and throws it across the room. Mama Tahiya and I jump up off the bed. She opens the door and pushes me into the hall, then shuts the door behind me.

I run to our room. Crashing and banging sounds come from their room. A moment of silence passes. Mama Tahiya's voice rises up: "Ayyy!" I push on our door and go in. Father stands in the doorway to the balcony. I call to him: "Papa, hurry. Uncle is beating Mama Tahiya."

He turns around and comes to me. We go out of the room and head towards the other one without talking. Sounds of "Ays" come one after another. Father listens in a trance. He pulls me by the hand to go back to our room. He closes the door behind us. He smiles and says: "Those aren't the sounds of a beating."

He prepares *sakhina* with warm milk for our evening meal. He boils some fenugreek. Adds molasses. The bread is cut into croutons. He throws it in a pan. Simmers it over a fire. He adds the fenugreek and molasses. Stirs it several times. He dishes it on to my plate and pours warm milk over it. I eat with a spoon while sitting on the edge of the bed. *He raises the seat until it is level with the table top. Mother covers my chest with a bib that she ties behind my neck. She puts a bowl of soup in front of me. She gives me my tiny spoon. They sit on either side of me.*

He turns off the light then comes back. He tells me to prepare my satchel and get ready for bed. He goes with me to the toilet. The door to the constable's room is open a crack. The sounds of the radio broken up by static come from behind it. Um Zakiya's radio is turned up. "Oh warriors in God's tour. This is the day you've longed for." I repeat the rest along with the radio: "We're the creators of the art of war."

Mama Tahiya moves across the living room. She is wearing a sleeveless, yellow silk dress. She is carrying a white handbag. A folded sweater rests on her arm. "Kareem" comes after her wearing a white shirt and grey trousers. A small hand towel in the palm of his hand flashes out from under his left sleeve like a flower. The two of them say "hi" to father. They leave the apartment. I settle into bed. Father sits in his full suit at my desk. He's wearing his glasses and holding a book in his hand. Sleep starts to overtake me. I can sense that he wants to go out. I decide not to doze off until he takes off his clothes.

The voice of Hajj Abdel 'Alim comes up from the alley: "Khalil Bey! Khalil Bey!" Father opens the glass door to the balcony and tells him to come up. He opens the door for him. Offers him the desk chair. He himself sits on the edge of the bed. As always, the sheikh of the quarter starts clearing his throat. He says that Abbas has married and brought his wife from his home village. She is a nice, innocent girl. She might be able to clean up for us and do the cooking. Father says: "That would be great."

Abdel 'Alim asks: "Have you been outside today? The streets are full of protests and people chanting: 'Where's our food, clothes, and basic things, thou most womanizing of all kings?'"

Father says: "They're really raising the stakes."

"The papers are calling them, 'our first fighters.' Refaat Effendi was in Port Said yesterday and he says that it's full of Palestinians running from the Zionist forces."

"How is Maged Effendi?"

Abdel 'Alim says that Zeraksh became pregnant and took him away to the kingdom of genies, so she could give birth there. She had the child without help from anyone and he walked the moment he came out of her.

Father asks with interest: "What did he see there?"

"They don't have either streetcars or buses up there. There's neither birds, nor animals, nor insects, nor cemeteries. Their digestive systems are like car engines. When they shit—excuse the expression—it comes out as steam flowing from their backsides exactly like car exhaust."

"So why did he come back? He'd be right to just stay there."

"He was choking from the lack of oxygen, so he told her he wanted to come back. She had him stand on top of her feet and put his hands on top of her head. She puffed out her cheeks and he suddenly found himself back in his own bed."

"Just like that? And nothing happened to him?"

"He just has a slight headache all the time and stumbles every now and then when he's walking."

Father asks about Abdel 'Alim's children. He answers: "The girl had a fever last night. I telephoned a doctor. He sat there and asked about my work and where we lived and then demanded three pounds for a house call."

"Good God! What did you do?"

"The Lord provided. I gave her two aspirin and made her a cold compress. By morning she was better."

He says he has come to visit father to ask a favor.

"At your service, inshallah."

He says that Hajj Mishaal had trumped up a drugs charge against him and he needs father to testify for him in the case.

Father says right away: "I'm happy to help. What happened exactly?"

"He took the shop across from mine and wants to buy mine also, but I didn't want to sell."

He stands up saying: "I have to go by the shop now. Did you

notice the loudspeaker that Mishaal has hung up?"

"Yeah. It reaches all the way to here. It doesn't let me sleep."

"Are you going to sit with us tonight? Um Kalthoum is sing-ing *The New Moon Has Risen*." Father turns toward me then says: "I'll have to see."

'Abdel Alim goes out. I sit up and say to him: "Papa, don't leave me alone." He studies me for a second then says: "Okay, get up and put your clothes on."

I get dressed in a hurry. I wipe off the lenses of my glasses with a handkerchief. We go out into the alley. Siham looks out of her window as usual. We go out to the main street and head toward Sikakny Square. After crossing several more wide streets, we make it to Cinema Rialto. The crowded foyer. A whistle, noises and shouting. We climb up a short staircase to a raised viewing stand at the back. We sit on a wooden bench. The man selling pumpkin seeds, peanuts, and pretzels goes from bench to bench. *I want to sit on her lap but she pushes me away from her. My father takes me between his knees. A seller passes by in a clean gallabiya with a basket covered by a cloth. He buys a giant pretzel with sesame for each of us. The vendor gives us each a bite-sized slice of Egyptian Romano wrapped in a paper.*

Father buys me a tube of roasted seeds. A double feature. First there's a short feature. It's an episode of the adventures of Jesse James. The main feature is *Bulbul Effendi*, starring the singers Farid Al-Atrash and Sabah.

The screen goes dark suddenly and the lights come up. Shouts go up. Father takes off his fez and his bald head shines in the light. He lights a cigarette. *Cinema Hillal in Sayida Zainab Square. I am with 'Azmy, the son of the maid of Mama Basima. We stand at the ticket window. The ticket seller wears a complete, fancy suit with a tilted fez. We don't have enough for the tickets. He waves at us to sneak in through the third-class door. We stop close to the screen. It is filled with the face of Laila Murad.*

The hall goes dark. The film starts up again. The air inside is choking. Father takes off his coat. The movie ends and lights shine. His face is frowning. He wipes the sweat from his brow and forces his lips into a smile. We wait for the crowds pushing through the exit to disperse. He takes my hand in his strong grip. We go out into the street. He buys me a semolina cake from the sweet shop. We walk slowly. Our alley is drowned in darkness. The entrance to the house, too. I hang on to his coat. His arms wrap around me.

We wash for prayer together. He lays out a blanket over the floor. While holding on to a long string of prayer beads, he sits on the blanket cross-legged. A frown. He recites the invocation. He repeats it as he counts off the beads on the string. He calls it "the millennial" because it has a thousand beads. The sound of the Friday sermon comes from Um Zakiya's radio. The sermon ends. I pray with him. The prayer is over, but he continues with a few extra bows. He tries to make sure I'm clean. He says I can't go to the bathroom for the next hour. He warns me not to answer if the doorbell rings or if anyone knocks on our door. He says that Abbas's wife has said she'll come this afternoon.

He closes the door of the balcony firmly then stuffs a piece of cloth at the bottom. Another piece under the door to the room. He puts the primus stove down on the floor at the edge of the blanket. On top of the flame, he sets a sheet of tin that he made from the lid of a can of shortening. He throws some frankincense, seeds and herbs on top of it from small bags lined up on the desk next to a white plate made of china. He pulls down the book *The Great Star of Knowledge*. The fragrant vapors rise up and fill the room. I cough. He mutters to himself the ninety-nine names of God. He brings a sheet of paper and ink. He sits cross-legged. He throws more of the incense on to the fire. He recites: "Say, 'I seek refuge in the Lord of the dawn/From the evil in His creation/From the evil of the dark as it spreads/From the evil of the sorceress who casts her breath on the knot/From the evil of the envious one who envies.'" I study the fire. He pokes me with his elbow so I'll repeat the verse. We recite it several times.

He takes a pin and a sheet of paper. He pokes it and says: "Against Nabila's eye. Against her husband's eye. Against Tahiya's eye. Against the constable's eye. Against 'Abdel Alim's eye. Against Ali Safa's eye. Against Um Safwat's eye. Against Hikmet's eye. Against Sheikh Afifi's eye." He thinks for a second, then adds: "Against Khalil's eye." He throws the paper on to the fire and watches it go up in flames.

I try to get up but he says we aren't done yet. He takes the china plate from on top of the desk. He puts it in front of himself. He takes the bottle of blue ink and a reed pen. He opens *The Great Star of Knowledge* to a page marked by a white sheet of paper. He sticks the pen in the bottle of ink. He grabs the plate and starts to write out the *fatiha* around its edges. He turns the plate around in a circle and keeps on until he has finished the whole chapter. He reads from the marked page of the book. He takes from it a big square with long columns covering it lengthwise and across the width. He pours a cup of water on to the dish and adds a few drops from the bottle of rose water and a spoon of honey. He gives it to me to drink. I pull my head away. He shouts at me: "Drink it!"

I drink the mixture. He tells me to repeat after him: "May God bless what I have drunk that it might help me with learning and comprehension." He reads from the *The Embryo*: "Recite in the name of thy Lord who created; created the human from an embryo. Recite and thy Lord is all giving, who taught by the pen, who taught the human what is known." He prostrates himself in prayer twice, and I pray with him. *My mother's voice from the bedroom: "Ya Seen, and the Quran is wisdom. Verily you are one of its messengers."* He puts the small shaving mirror in my hand. He tells me to press my finger on its brass frame that keeps falling off.

He opens the book to another page. He says that the exam questions are going to appear on the mirror's glass and that I need to pay close attention. He reads from the book in a voice that shakes: "O Lord, employ Your angels on my behalf, there is no god but You, O Lord of dignity and generosity, O living and ascendant One I implore You, Giver of sustenance to sustain me." He repeats the incantation forty times while counting on his fingers. He says: "O Answerer, answer my call and fulfill my needs."

I stare at the surface of the mirror and repeat after him: "I ask You by Boqallim, Shounahil, Shahareen, I ask You by the holiness of Kashheel, Bardeem, Baha'eel, Ajajeel, 'Anaseel, and I ask You by the holiness of Gabrael, Micha'il, Israfeel, and Az-ra'el. O Lord, I ask You verily O Lord of dignity and generosity, O living and ascendant One. I ask in Your name, O most supreme One." He scolds me: "Slow down." He continues: "And I ask You in your name, Allah, Allah, Allah, the Beautiful, the Generous, and I ask You in Your name, the One, the Glorious, and I ask You in Your name, God the Prince of holiness and peace, the Trustworthy, the beloved Grand Ruler, the grace of Allah fall on our pleas. If You should come to us conveyor of these names, answer us with the righteousness of He who speaks the heavens and earth, may our will and our obedience come to us and speak, addressing us in our obedience, in the rightness of A'aya, Sharaahiya, Adotay, Usbawat, with haste, with haste, right now, right now."

He asks me: "Did anything come up?"

I answer: "I'm not sure. There's some scribbling in the corner."

He sounds worried as he asks: "In English?"

"Don't know."

He takes it from me. He studies it then gives it back to me saying that the scribbling is just a rust spot. He reads the book and then flips through a few pages.

"Did anything come up?"

I shake my head. He says sadly: "I don't know what happened. Are you sure that you've washed?" I say I'm sure and he shakes his head like he's all confused.

He flips through the book then stops at one of the pages. He takes a sheet of paper and writes a few words on it. He folds it up and hands it to me: "Keep this in your pocket always."

I want to get up. He stops me: "Memorize that invocation. Say it with me." He recites: "By the right of these noble names, Kahi'adh, hem 'asiq. Dumb and deaf and blind, for they will not return to Him." I repeat the invocation after him. He tests me. He makes sure I know it by heart. He tells me to recite it seventy times as I enter the oral exam. Then I repeat the word "Kahi'adh" letter by letter. After each letter, I curl up a finger from my right hand. When my turn comes before the examiner, I raise up my hand, unfolding them in his face. *The magician takes out his things and spreads them around in a big circle. We gather around the circle. He pulls a long chain of colored handkerchiefs from his sleeve. He raises a bottle of gas to his mouth. He takes up a long steel pole with a flame burning at the end of it. He opens his mouth and blows up a flame like a rocket launching. He promises us we'll see a snake coming out of its egg if we pay him. He passes through us holding a tambourine with his monkey tied to him by a chain. He finishes the pass through then shakes the tambourine. He announces that what he has collected isn't enough. He takes his things and leaves.*

Chapter Three

S he unfolds the sheets and pillows over the edge of the balcony. He screams at her: "The mattress first." She drags the sheets and pillows to the side. She comes back into the room and bends over the mattress. He helps her lift it on top of her head. Her frail body wavers. She throws it on top of the balcony ledge and rains down blows with the wicker dust racket. Thick dust floats up from it. She beats the blankets and the pillows. She starts to pant from the work and her pale face turns red.

She drags the bed frame away from the wall. She lights the primus stove, then carries it in her hand and bends over the metal box springs. She holds shut the opening of her *gallabiya* that almost exposes her breasts. Father puts on his glasses. He tells her: "Give it to me." He takes the burner from her and squats down next to the frame. He sets the stove under the hole that the box springs rest in. I lean over next to him. I study his strong hands that hold on to the stove so firmly. I notice some bedbugs in a row. The fire touches them and they burst into flames and fall to the ground. I point out one that is getting away. He catches up to it with the flame. He turns around with the stove and goes to the other side of the frame. She brings him a bottle of paraffin and he pours from it on to the burnt spots. He tells us to look carefully around the sides of the mattress and the folds of the pillows.

"Give me the jug."

She brings a jug of water from the living room. He sips from it, then wipes his lips with the sleeve of his *gallabiya*. He says: "It's hot. Put it on top of the sideboard in the breeze." She says: "Shall I go get some ice, Sidi?" As she speaks, her mouth opens and shows her yellow teeth. He answers: "No. Not now." *The ice seller is at the door. He's carrying half a block wrapped in canvas. He puts it on top of the dinner table. Mother carries it to the kitchen. She breaks off a piece with the handle of the wooden pestle, then bangs at it to make smaller pieces. She rinses it with water and scatters it over the plates of paluza, the white pudding, lined up on the top of the sideboard. We eat it sitting next to the window.*

He drags the desk chair over and stands on top of it. Gently, he brings over the wall clock. He hands it to Fatima as he says: "Take it easy. Be careful." She puts the clock over the frame of the bed. She brings a piece of cloth and wets it with the paraffin. She goes to clean off the clock, but he stops her and gets down. He takes the cloth from her. He wipes off the sides of the clock with it. He opens its glass pane. Wipes the edges around the clockwork. He asks her for the bottle and another piece of cloth. She gives him an old wool sock. He wets it with the paraffin. He takes hold of the pendulum and rubs it well. He carefully wipes off its roman numbers. Then he takes a small can about the size of his hand with a little spout on top. Puts the spout under the clockwork and tilts it to pour out what's inside. He pours into the two openings in the middle of the ring of numbers and wipes off a small, shiny brass opening. He presses it into one of the openings and turns it gently. Moves to the other one. Turns the key several times until it won't go any more.

He takes the clock to the hall and puts it above the table. His eyes move from one wall to another. He settles on a spot between the door on to the skylight and the door to the guest room. Fatima takes one of the dining chairs and brings it to the place he has fixed on. He climbs up on to the chair. He asks me for the hammer and a medium-sized nail. I run back to the room. I get down on my knees in front of the bed and pull out the hammer and a cardboard box from underneath it. The box is full of nails, bits of electric cord, tacks, and parts from light fixtures. I pick out some nails that are different sizes. I run back. Father stretches his hand out to me. Fatima snatches away the hammer and nails and hands them to him. He chooses one of the nails and pounds it into the wall. His strokes are strong and sure.

I go over to the door of the constable and Mama Tahiya. I look in the keyhole. There is no trace left of their bed or their chiffonier. They took all their furniture when they moved to their new place. Father shouts at me: "Where are you?" I rush back. He stretches out his hand with the hammer in it, but Fatima takes it before I can. The hammer almost falls between us and he tells me: "You're good for nothing." He asks her to gently bring him the clock. She brings it to him. He hangs it on the nail. He takes its pendulum from her and fixes it under the clockwork. He swings it on and the clock starts to work.

He closes the glass and climbs down.

We go back to the room. He asks her to take down the framed pictures. She gets up on the chair. Her scarf gets hung on the side of the wardrobe. She pulls it out and ties it again over her thick hair. Her *gallabiya* gathers up in her crack. She sticks her hand out and straightens it. Father's eyes fix on her small bottom. She takes down a picture and gives it to him. It's big, with a wide wooden frame and has small egg-shaped head shots in one row after another. I know father's picture is in the second row from the bottom. 'Azmi, the son of Mama Basima's cook, has taken it out once. Father dusts it off with a rag and puts it on top of the box.

She gives him another picture. It shakes in her hand. He yells at her: "Your hand's wobbly!" The picture shows him sitting in the middle of several army officers. Smiling in a fancy uniform. His shoes are shiny and have pointy ends. His hand is wrapped around a fly whisk that rests in his lap. His moustache turns up on the sides, like the moustache of King Fuad.

A third picture has a fine wooden frame with something that looks like a cross in each corner. He stands between two officers. One of them wears puffy pants tucked in high boots that come up to the knee. The shoulders of their uniforms have small, steel swords that show they're officers. He takes hold of the picture in his hand and stares up at the wall as if searching for a place to hang it. I say: "Shouldn't we put a glass pane over it first?" He shakes his head as if he's sad: "May God have vengeance on them." *Mama Basima with 'Azmi goes out all mad and leaves us with his mother, the cook. We start to gather up our things in canvas bags. He puts the big pictures in grooved frames in the bag and ties it with string. We stack what we need next to the door. We put on our clothes and get ready to leave. I go to the toilet to pee. I trip over the water bucket and it spills. The cook yells at me: "Are you blind?" He yells back at her: "Shut up!" She runs to the door. She opens it. She grabs one of the bags. She throws it over the ledge of the stairwell. She grabs another. We rush out and go down. The bag of pictures comes after us. It crashes at the bottom and I hear the sound of breaking glass.*

Fatima takes the pictures back to their place over the dresser. He points at a yellow envelope and asks her to bring it over. He throws it towards the desk and it falls. She starts to bring in the bedding.

We leave her alone in the room so she can sweep and mop it. Father brings the yellow envelope with him. He sits at the table in the hall facing the door to our room. I stand next to him. He dumps out what is in the envelope. Pictures without frames around them, some of them as small as a postcard. He picks up one and studies it. I lean over his shoulder. My glasses slide down my nose and I put them back in place. Father is between my aunt and my uncle's wife. They're all three wearing white *gallabiyas*. Only father, in his skull cap, wears anything on his head. The hair of my aunt and uncle's wife is black like charcoal. It's short and thick and gathered around their faces. Nabila is standing in front of my father's legs. Behind them, there's a wall made of reeds, and in front of them, a beach. I ask him: "Where's this?" He says: "In front of our cabin at Ras al-Bar."

He puts the picture to the side and picks up another. A crowded beach. Father, his face full of laughter, is in a white suit coat, a fez, and a necktie. He's holding a cigarette. I don't know any of the people in the crowd next to him except my

141

brother, who is wearing a bathrobe.

He stands up and goes to the entrance of our room. He follows Fatima as she bends over her squeegee. She stacks up the rag on its blade with her hands. He waves at her to unfold it and then fold it up again into one straight piece. She finishes cleaning the room. She sits down on the edge of the bed to change the sweaty pillow cases. I'm waiting uncomfortably for her to get up and move away from the bed. Father swats at the flies with a towel. She says that her husband bought a can of Mobiltox to kill insects, from the shop attached to the petrol station. Father says: "You mean you know about Mobiltox too?" She says: "So because I'm a *fellah* that means I'm ignorant?" She brings in the long rug that she hung over the ledge of the balcony. She asks my father: "Shall I spread it on the ground, Sidi?" He replies: "No. It's hot as hell. Fold it and put it under the bed."

The sound of the watermelon vendor comes in from the window. Father goes out to the balcony. He calls to him: "Are they ripe?" "Of course, Bey." The seller picks one up and thumps it with the flat of his hand. He puts it back and picks up another one. He thumps again. Father starts to say something, but the seller cuts into it with a knife. He makes a square opening in its side. He turns it over and pulls out a piece that is bright red, then he sticks it back into place. He puts it to the side and picks up another one. Father calls out: "One's enough." He bends over and takes the cut watermelon from him. He gives him his money. He takes it to the sink and washes off its surface, taking care not to get water in its opening. Then he puts it on a tray on top of the sideboard. He brings a piece of cheesecloth from the dresser and covers it.

We get ready to have lunch. Father notices that the okra in red sauce has turned sour. She says she forgot to boil it yesterday. I wait uneasily for father to explode, but he doesn't say a word. Instead he sends her to buy head meat from the Husseiniya market. I say: "Shall I go?" He says no. She goes to the storage room and comes back wrapped in her black coat. He gives her some money. He repeats to her: "Forehead, eye, brain, and tripe." He runs after her and yells down the stairwell: "Don't forget the pickles and arugula."

He takes the envelopes back to the room and throws them on top of the desk. I pick up a picture with some man wearing a big overcoat that goes down to his shoe tops. His fez covers his forehead and comes down almost all the way to his eyes. His thin moustache twists upwards. His right hand is behind his back and his left fist sits on the table. A big vase sits on the ground with the end of a curtain hanging on it. The picture is old and its edge is torn. I turn it over. Nothing. I show it to father. "Who's this?" He takes it and studies it for a while. He says: "It's me."

"You?"

"Yeah, when I was eighteen."

I show him another picture of a man in a winter coat. The fez is again close to the eyes and the moustache twisting upwards. He's sitting in a chair with his left elbow on an armrest that has a lion's head on the end of it. His thumb is propped against his cheek. The other hand has a cigarette holder between the index and middle fingers. The sleeve of his pressed shirt shows a button at his wrist. He says: "That's me too—

after I married Nabila's mother. I was about twenty-seven." I turn over the picture and read my father's full name written in red pencil. The handwriting is my mother's.

I recognize him easily in another picture. He's in a fancy suit, resting his hand on the handle of a walking stick. His back is leaning against a brick wall. He looks very handsome. There's a beautiful boy next to him in a suit with two rows of buttons. A folded handkerchief dangles from the breast pocket of his jacket. His short trousers stop just below the knee, at the tops of his long socks. I flip over the picture: "Respected Mr. Khalil Effendi with his son during Eid of 1928." Underneath is my brother's signature.

In the last picture, he looks the way he is now. He's sitting down, reading in a full suit. His fez tilts back. The glasses are sliding down his nose. The wrinkles in his neck show over the collar of his shirt. On the back of the picture, he's written in his own hand: "1945."

Fatima comes back with a wrapper full of head meat. She puts it in a plate on top of the table and takes the arugula to the kitchen. Father shouts at her: "Wash it well." He waves at her to come and eat with us. I get mad and think about not eating anything if she does come. She says she has to make tomorrow's food for her husband. He puts a piece of meat in a half loaf for her. She takes it and thanks him.

I get out of my chair and drag it to the table. I notice a small picture on the floor. It must have fallen from the envelope. A small girl wears a dress with short sleeves. Her face is round and her hair is curly. She has short boots on. Her right hand rests on her stomach and her left sits on a stone wall. There's a strange look in her eyes. Fear? Worry? Anger? I recognize father's neat handwriting on the back, "middle of 1921." I give it to father asking: "Who's this picture of?"

He answers curtly: "Your mother." *I stand on top of a chair in my white summer pyjamas with their short sleeves. My elbows are leaning against the windowsill. I watch the people walking. The sun moves close to the edge of the window. I jump down to the floor and go out to the hall. The voice of mother comes from the kitchen, singing: "I'm going to hide my pain."*

We get off the tram at the Lazoghly Square stop. I stare at the head of the statue wrapped in its big turban. We pass in front of a grand café with shiny mirrors covering its walls. The café's at the corner of two streets that come to a dead end in the square. Two of father's friends wave at him and invite him to join them. He signals to them that he's headed to the next building, and that he will pass by them on the way back.

We cross the street to an old building. We go in through an open door. We walk through a long hallway crowded with old men. There is an old man in a full suit. He's shorter than father. He leans on a stick and has trouble walking. His face is so white it hits you. White hair appears at the rim of his fez. We get close to him and try to go around him, but he stops father. Father looks at him surprised. He says to father in a shaky voice: "Khalil Effendi? I am Rifqy." Father greets him a little embarrassed and says: "How are you, Rifqy Bey?" "As you can see." Father says: "May God give you health." The old man looks at me and asks: "Your grandson?" "No, my son." "God does provide! How are his exams going? God willing, he's passing them?" Father says: "He has an English makeup exam."

We leave him and keep on walking. Father's steps slow down. The smile that he had drawn on to his lips as we went out disappears. We stand in a queue that ends at a glass window that has the word "cashier" written in cursive script that forms a circle, and underneath it is a foreign word.

A man with a thick laughing face comes up to us. He greets father warmly. He asks him why he doesn't come to the meetings of the group. Father makes excuses about the duties of daily life. He asks him what happened with the special lawsuit over the partial liquidation of retirements. The man shakes his head unhappily: "It looks like there's no hope. The government's dead set on stealing from us." "What can we do?" "We have to retain a big shot lawyer."

The queue moves. We find ourselves in front of the window. Father takes the withdrawal slip for his retirement payment out of the jacket of his suit coat. He gives it to the clerk sitting behind the window. The clerk hands several pounds over to him. Father signs a receipt of acknowledgment.

We leave the building. We cross the street. I'm expecting that he'll go to the café, but he walks around it. He goes through a small alley across the way. We end up in the street with the tram line and wait on the platform at the station. We get on. We get off at Attaba Square. I know it by the white firehouse with the red trucks sitting in its driveway.

We cross the square to the huge building that is facing us. It has a round dome at the top. I say that I'm thirsty. The *araqsoos* vendor stands in our way, clanging together his castanets. *I drag one of the folding chairs to the window and climb up on it. The* araqsoos *vendor comes out of the side alley. His clothes are white and clean. The*

Father takes off his fez. Wipes the sweat off his bald head with a handkerchief. He sips a bit from the beer mug then lights a cigarette. I take a piece of bread, plunge it into the tahini, and gobble it up. I pick at the dish of peanuts. A vendor comes by in a *gallabiya* carrying a small basket full of boiled prawns. Father shakes his head to say no. Another vendor follows selling lottery tickets. Father takes a notebook from him that has schedules of numbers. He takes a lottery ticket out of his suit jacket pocket. He searches for its numbers in the register. Then he gives it back to the vendor with a sad smile. He takes some tickets from him and chooses one. He pays him a piastre. The shoeshine man comes over to us. He sits down at father's feet. Father puts his right foot up on the step of the shine box.

I stare at the high counter with many men standing around it. A row of colored bottles is behind it. I see an old man who looks like a foreigner in fancy clothes stretched out on the floor next to the counter. He keeps repeating words that make the men, who are standing, laugh. No one bothers to help him get up. *The small bottle on the table has a lot of plates spread around it. Smell of sautéed liver. The room is empty. Mother's voice comes from the bedroom: "Darling come and save me, see what I've been through. "My father's voice finishes the lyrics: "I've been crushed by passion for you."*

The shoeshine finishes the right shoe and taps on the wooden box. Father puts down his right foot and lifts up his left. I take the last piece of bread and use it to wipe clean the plate of tahini. The shoeshine finishes up. Father gives him half a piastre. He raises his mug of beer to his lips. He swallows its last drops slowly. The waiter comes back and asks father if he wants anything else. He shakes his head. We pay and leave.

We catch the tram, riding in the closed car. There's an empty seat next to a man in a caftan and a country style skull cap. I ride on father's lap. The back of the seat in front of us is in my face. A woman in a black cloak is sitting on it, next to a girl wearing a blouse and skirt. The woman has taken over the space that separates the chairs. Her thighs hang over the edge of the seat a little. A man in a suit and fez comes by. He stands next to her seat. He leans over and rests his hand on the back of the chair. His knee is very close to the upper part of the woman's thigh.

I look out of the window at the cinema billboards. The tramcar rocks from side to side. I turn back around to the front. I notice the man's knee rubbing against the woman's leg. She leans over to her friend and they exchange whispers. The man rubs his knee on her thigh. I look up at his face. He stares back at me. I turn my eyes back to the window. I pretend to stare at the street, but I can see her from the corner of my eye, leaning further toward her friend. The man's knee is almost right on her crack. I look up at his face. He stares straight back. His look sets on me, so I turn away. The tram stops. The woman gets up in a hurry. She says goodbye to her friend. She avoids looking at the man. She pushes her way quickly through the passengers who are standing and heads toward the door. Her cloak is caught up in her crack. One of the people standing up takes her seat. The man's face is pale. There are beads of sweat on his forehead. He bends over to look out of the window of the tramcar, then stands back up straight. He looks around. Our eyes meet. He stares hard. I turn my eyes away.

We get off the tramcar in the square. We cross it to go over to the Dukhakhny shop at the corner of Farouk and al-Zaher streets. Father buys a pack of his cigarettes with the yellow package and the picture of the Ethiopian head. We circle the square and cross the street that leads to our old house. We come to the Um 'Abbas fountain. One of the passers-by drinks from its tap. I look towards the street that goes up to our old house. The florist stands on the corner. The horse's head is buried in his sack of feed. Three street sweepers with their yellow clothes, bushy moustaches, and long brooms are at work. Their caps are turned backward, for the brims to shade the back of their necks. *He pounds the broom's handle on the ground to fix its head back on. Dust comes off it. The head falls off the handle again. He sits down on the pavement. He fastens a piece of a rag between the head and the stick.*

We cross the street. We make it to Abdel Malik bakery. We head for the pharmacy. Father pushes the dark glass door. The breeze from the circular ceiling fan hits us. The pharmacist is wearing glasses with big thick lenses. Father asks about his account. The chemist flips through pages of his register. Father pays him a chunk of what he owes. He promises to pay the rest at the beginning of next month. He leans to him and whispers something. The man smiles and says: "I wish. Try taking some Vitamin B." Father buys two small bottles—one with tincture of iodine, the other mercurochrome.

We go back to Nuzha Street. We stop in front of the butcher. Father buys a pound of kidneys and sheep's testicles. He pays last month's bill. He asks: "What's new with your father?"

He answers in a disapproving voice: "He's with his bride."

Father smiles: "Congratulations."

"Is it right for an old man to do that?"

"Well, how old is he?"

"He's past sixty."

Father shakes his head: "Is he planning to have a kid?"

"No, thank God. She can't have children. But he wants to bequeath the shop to her."

We buy a melon from a horse-drawn cart. We cross the street to Hajj Abdel 'Alim's shop. We go in. Salim opens the register as soon as he sees father. We settle up with him. Father asks for a little bit of raw sugar. Salim asks him in a dry tone: "How much, then?"

"Fifty dirham. To sweeten the melon."

We head toward the alley. Father says to me: "By now, Fatima's made the rice and green beans." I say: "She can't make rice the way you can."

The afternoon call to prayer echoes loudly from Hajj Mishaal's megaphone hung at the end of the alleyway. The iron salesman looks out from the balcony of his second wife. He rests his arms on its edge. Signs of being mad show on his face. He stretches out his right hand, holding the end of a black rubber hose. He points its spout toward the place where we've dug out five circles for our game of marbles. The water shoots out from the spout of the hose. It rains over the grooves for the marbles and washes them away. We gather the marbles. Everyone takes his own. Safwat goes up to his apartment. Samir and I stand there all confused. His face is full of pock marks, just like his mother's. The water runs through the alley and washes away any chance for us to keep playing. Father calls me from the balcony. I go up. I wash my face and feet under the tap. I go back to the room and dry off my face with the towel hanging from the edge of the bed. *As the sun disappears, he calls to me. I hurry inside and go to the bathroom right away. I wash my face and my feet. I catch up with him at the window. The darkness swallows us. We sit in the dark without turning on the light. The street is quiet; there's no one around.*

I open the left door of the cupboard. I reach for the travel bag. I pull out a handful of hazelnuts, walnuts, and almonds. I put them on the desk. I open the right door. I take out a roll of dried apricot. I cut off a slice the size of my hand. I look around for the nutcracker until I find it buried under some clothes. I sit at the desk. I open the book of Layla Murad songs. I break open two hazelnuts, two almonds, and a walnut. I take a small bit of apricot and suck on it while I add hazelnut and almond. Father goes to and fro from the balcony to the door of the room. He groans from the awful heat. He says over and over: "Let it keep getting hotter, until it has to finally break!" He drives away the flies for the umpteenth time. A familiar voice comes up from the alley. "Shakookoo! For a bottle!" I run to the balcony. The call is repeated from a man with a cart full of small plaster statues of the famous singer and comedian. I turn around to ask father for an empty bottle that I can exchange for one of the statues. His frowning face does not give me much hope.

A vendor calls out from the entrance to the alley: "Almonds!" Father calls out to Fatima. She appears at the door to the room, wiping her hands off on her *gallabiya*. He asks her what she is doing. She answers: "I'm chopping *mulukhiya*, Sidi." He turns to me saying: "Take a piastre out of my pocket and go and bring a pound of dates." I grab for his suit coat on its hanger in the corner. I root around in its pocket until I find the change. I pull out a fistful and pick out a piastre from it. I take two millimes also. I ask him: "How much should I pay?" He says: "Pay what he asks for. *You* can't barter." I head towards the door and he calls to me: "Pay attention to the scale. Don't let him cheat you."

I leave the apartment at a run. I cut across the alleyway to get to the street. The date seller is sitting on one of the arms of his cart with a leg propped up on the other one. His feet are bare and dirty. The dates are stacked up in a round basket made of palm leaves. It is covered with a thin white cloth. He pulls the covering down a bit and grabs some dates with his hand. He puts them on one side of the scale. I walk around him to be closer to it and make sure it's okay. He makes a cone out of paper and then pours the stack of dates into it. He throws in two more dates. He hands me some change from the piastre. I run over to the nut seller and buy a millime's worth of melon seeds and another of chickpeas.

I go out again right before sundown to buy *ful* beans for our *suhur*, the late night snack during Ramadan. The seller is standing behind his kettle at the entrance to the alleyway. A crowd of boys and girls surrounds him. Their hands are all stretched out with plates and pots. They're all calling for him to serve them next. We're all excitedly following the movement of his right hand out of the kettle with its ladle full of beans. I start to call out with them as I stretch out the empty plate in my right hand and the money in my left. Their voices are louder than mine.

By the time I get my beans and go back, reading from the Quran has started. Its sound comes at us from two directions: the megaphone of Hajj Mishaal and the radio of Um Zakiya. Father is soaking two dry Nubian dates in a cup of water. Fatima finishes chopping the *mulukhiya*. She puts it on the fire and starts to peel off a few garlic cloves to make the broth. Father warns her not to start sautéing the mix right away.

He says that Um Nabila, God rest her soul, use to get ready to sauté the *mulukhiya* the moment she heard his steps in the stairwell, but she would not actually do it until after he sat at the table, so that he could smell it.

He washes for prayer and gets ready. The reciter ends the reading with "Believe in the Supreme God." A quiet moment passes. We wait anxiously. The cannon at the citadel fires to signal that it is sundown. Its boom echoes from the radio and the megaphone. The sunset call to prayer follows. Father picks up the cup of dates and sips from it slowly. He takes a bite of a date. He spreads the prayer rug out over the floor. He prays the *maghrib*. Fatima sautés the *mulukhiya*. She brings the pan to the round table. She follows it up with a pot of rice and two plates. "Do you want anything else?" As he recites Quran, father raises his voice to drive her away. She says: "Okay. I'm going." She runs out in a hurry. Father finishes his prayer. The light of the day's end breaks up quickly. The electric lamp shines. He sits at the edge of the bed. I sit on the chair in front of him. He serves me *mulukhiya* with the ladle. He adds a piece of meat to it. I tear off a piece from the loaf of bread. I dip it in the *mulukhiya*. He serves himself. A complete silence descends over the alley. Sound of a spoon clanging against a plate. The sound is so close, it is as if it's in our apartment.

All of a sudden, the alarm siren goes off. Voices from outside: "Put out the light." I slide the chair back. I run to the light switch and turn it off. Darkness swallows us. Father stands up. He calls me. I answer: "I'm here, papa." He reaches out his hand and takes me into a hug. We turn towards the balcony. We move close to it. The siren stops sounding. A total silence falls. He says: "Those dogs! The truce hasn't ended yet." He reaches his hand out to shut the door to the balcony. Then he goes back and opens it again. He says: "The glass could break."

I move closer. The alley is swallowed in darkness. I stretch my neck to look up. The warplanes cut through the sky at a feverish speed. Two of them linger over a spot of light. They move away. All at once, they disappear. The sound of a faint and distant explosion resounds. His hand comes down on my shoulder harshly. He says: "Come back in here where it's safer."

He pulls off a blanket from on top of the bed. He crawls underneath it. He pushes away the old suitcase and spreads the blanket out over the floor. I do as he does. He gets down on his knees, leaning forward so his head does not hit the box springs. I huddle next to him. He wraps his arm around me.

I crawl to the edge of the bed near the door to the balcony. I stick my head out and look up at the piece of the sky that I can see. One of the stars fades away quickly. The ground defense searchlights gather together and try to catch it. Father whispers: "Where did you go? Come back here." I go back next to him. We wait in the quiet. A ringing sound draws near. It gets closer and grows loud. Suddenly, it stops. I hear the sound of an explosion. *The alarm siren comes on and off. My father switches off the light. Mother refuses to go to the storage closet. He begs her. She shouts back at him: "Is the closet going to protect us? Wake up, man. God is the Protector." We sit in the living room. He takes me in his arms. The sound of cannons goes off every few minutes. A faint and familiar whistle. It gets closer and louder. It stops. A German bomb lands in front of the building. The glass in the window to the skylight shakes. The sideboard rocks forward. The mirror mounted on top of it falls off.*

After a while, the all-clear siren goes off. My father gets up to turn on the light while he mutters thanks and praise to God. Mother's face is so white it's scary.

I grab hold of father. He hugs me. He crawls out from under the bed and I follow him. We leave the room and go to the hall. We head towards the bathroom. He goes into the toilet. Water runs out of the tap in a strained trickle. He gathers up his *gallabiya* and leans forward. He presses the tap shut, and takes out a box of matches from his pocket. Strikes a match. The round circle of the toilet appears in the light. He raises the match up and climbs up on the stone base. I hang on to his *gallabiya*. He stretches out his hand and pulls me to him. I look away towards the wall. I close my eyes. I try to ignore the rotten smell of the toilet. I bury my face in his *gallabiya*. I listen to the sound of his breathing. My ear rubs against a piece of metal in his hernia belt. The sounds of explosions go on. He shivers. He shouts out: "O Gentle One, be gentle."

I see after a while that the explosions have stopped. He loosens his grip on my shoulder. Silence starts to settle in. Then a long all-clear siren goes off. His panting settles down. We go out to the hallway. He turns on the light in the living room. We go back into our room. He turns on the light. He lights a black cigarette. We forget about the food and stand on the balcony. The children of the neighborhood come out carrying Ramadan lamps. Sameer carries a lamp with oval-shaped sides. Each side is a different color. Someone else has a lamp shaped like a football. I come back into the room and grab my lamp from on top of the desk. Its side panels are square. I open the main one and light the wick. I close it and it comes back open. I close it harder. I carry it very gently from the ring of tin at its top so I don't get poked by the sharp edges of its base. I go out on to the balcony.

I watch the children as they chant: "*Halloo, ya halloo!* Ramadan has come, *ya halloo!*" In the middle of their chants, I can hear Samir's delicate voice cutting through the others singing: "*Wahawee, ya wahawee! eeyooha!*" They're coming out from deep inside the alley. They make it to underneath our balcony and one of them calls out: "O you fast-breaker! O you duty shaker!" Does he mean us? They pass on, further down the alley.

He prays the evening prayer. We put on our clothes to go out. He wraps his brown shoes, with the white tips, in a newspaper. He also rolls up the piece of brown cloth that we bought from the constable. We leave the house. We go out all the way to the street, passing in front of the sheikh of the quarter's shop. There's no one inside except Saleem, who stands behind the counter. We stop at the shoe repair shop. He hands over the shoes. The shoe repairman turns them in his hand and says: "The sole's worn out. At the front and the back."

Father says: "Put a piece of metal at the front and make it into a half sole."

"Listen to my advice. Make a whole new sole. This is English. You don't want to give it up."

"Like I said, metal and a half sole."

"Okay. Do you know how much new shoes are running these days, Bey? There's a new American brand at Nasif for 68 piastres."

"But it won't last more than a couple of wearings ... American."

He turns towards me saying: "Have you bought your shoes for the feast?"

Father answers before I can: "We're waiting for the big feast, *Inshallah.*"

He heads for the wooden newspaper rack. He unfolds today's paper and reads through the headlines. I press my head between his stomach and the newspaper. The king in his dark glasses during a visit to the military hospital comforts the wounded returning from the front. The king of Transjordan is with him. Behind them are the two princesses, Fawziya and Faiza, in military clothes. Fawziya is a three-star general and Faiza a one-star. The shoe repairman says that we've become involved in a war that's none of our business.

We keep walking to the square and then turn right and go down Qamr Street. We stop at the tailor's shop. He sits in front of the shop on a chair with his legs stretched over another one. He's working on repairing a jacket. Father gives him the cloth and says: "We want to make a suit for Eid out of it." He studies the cloth, then says: "But Khalil Bey, this cloth is for curtains."

"For curtains or not for curtains, I'm asking if you can do it.

The tailor nods his head, but he is not happy. He takes my measurements. Short trousers down to the knee. We agree that we will come back in a week to make the first patterns. We leave him and keep walking until we make it to Sakakeeny Square. We pass by the church. We go through Tourseena Street until it dead ends into al-Nuzha. Father stops in front of the villa of his friend, General Fareed. He pushes on the iron gate and I follow him up a path that cuts through a well-kept front yard. As we go up the few steps, he scrapes his shoes against the marble to announce that he is there. He knocks on an iron door. An old maid opens the door for us. He asks: "Is the bey here?" She invites him to come in.

We stop in an entrance hall crowded with furniture over a thick rug. She disappears then comes back. "Please come in, Bey." We follow her to the guest room. Pictures of military officers, like the ones in our house, hang on the walls. A huge chandelier hangs from the ceiling. The general shows up after a while. He is wearing a robe made from colored silk and he is leaning on a cane. "Welcome, Khalil Bey. What a nice surprise!" He sits next to us and rests his cane between his legs. His face is dark and he has a sunken spot right under his neck. I know that it is from being shot. He's wearing a white shirt under his robe with a stiff collar that the dead skin in his neck hangs over. His moustache is huge with big, woolly halves hanging down. He calls to the maid and asks her to bring the dishes of Ramadan fruit from the refrigerator. She brings three dishes on a round tray. Father gives me a dish and takes one for himself. He seems pleased with the cool dish. *Mother lines up the small dishes of Ramadan fruit on the marble on top of the sideboard. She breaks up the ice into pieces with a wooden adze. She sprinkles it over the dishes.*

They chat about the air raid. Father says that we were wrong to accept the truce. The general says that we had to accept it because our recent losses had been so awful. An example was the siege of Faluja. The Jewish forces kept our troops from getting water to the point that they ended up drinking their own piss. He mocked the talk between the defense minister, Haydar Pasha, and one of the other ministers that had been reported in the papers. The minister was supposed to have said to him: "Go for it, pasha. Let's spend our Eid in Tel Aviv." The general commented: "Yeah, right. I'll be sure to meet you there."

Their talk moves on to the housing crisis. Father says: "Can you imagine that some apartments require an advance of 300 pounds, non-refundable." The general picks up a picture magazine and says: "Did you see the sentence for the killing of Amin Othman? Anwar Sadat was found innocent." He puts the magazine down and says: "He was an officer in my unit. I didn't like him at all. He was slippery." I pick up the magazine. I look at the picture of Sadat. His clothes are elegant. The knot of his necktie is weirdly small. His head and beard are neatly groomed. The barber had followed the trend of shaving off all the hair around the ears.

The general calls the maid and asks her to go find his two boys. They're big and tall. They stand in fear at the doorway. The bigger one asks: "Did you want something, sir?" He orders them to play with me. We move to another guest room. All three of us sit on a thick, dark red carpet. The maid brings in a big tray of dried fruit and nuts. I grab a hazelnut and the nutcracker. They start up a two-way card game that is too fast for me to follow. The bigger one suggests they bet on whether Abou Hebaga will win at the London Olympics at the end of the month. I ask: "Who's Abou Hebaga?" The smaller one says: "Can anyone not know the hero of Ahly Sporting Club?" His brother backs him up: "The greatest football player in the world!"

I get up and walk around the room. I sit on a couch. It has comfortable cushions dyed in dark colors. Pictures of the boys with their father and other relatives are hanging on the wall. I get up. The two boys are lost in their game. I sneak out of the guest room and into the living room. It is dark. At one end there's a lighted room. I move close to it. I hear the sound of Quranic recitation. I peek in with care. A sheikh wearing a turban and a flowing cloak sits cross-legged on an oriental couch. His hand is on his cheek. He recites while rocking himself to the left and right. As the verse ends, he continues the rocking silently. I go back to the living room. The big boy suggests that we play hearts.

Father appears at the door with the general behind him. I follow him outside. We leave the villa and make our way back to the house. He stops us at the house and home shop. We buy a box of small glass teacups with colored inscriptions decorating its sides. He sets it on top of the sideboard and says that they are for Eid.

The calls of the yoghurt seller float up to us. He grabs an empty, brown-colored clay pot. We go into our room and open the door to the balcony. He calls to the vendor and hands him the pot. The vendor takes out a full container from the bottom covered with white cloth. He hands it up to father.

In the distance, the voice of the crier waking people up for the pre-dawn meal echoes through the quarter: "Wake up, sleepers in the night; make your stomachs full and right!" The sound of his drumbeats comes closer. He enters our alley. His face is hidden by the darkness. He stops in front of each house and calls on the people living in them by name. A tap of the drum comes after each name. He calls out Father's name and then mine.

Father makes a plate of fried eggs. I ask him: "Where's Fatima?" He says, "She's celebrating Eid."

We have our breakfast in the living room. He brings the teapot and pours some into two of our new glasses. He adds sugar and stirs. When I pick my cup up, the base of it breaks off and hot tea spills over the table. When he takes his cup, the same thing happens. He stands up and leaves everything sitting on the table. We go to wash our hands.

He drags the desk chair out to the balcony. Lights a cigarette. He asks me to look for a paper and something to write with. I bring him my homework notebook and my pencil. He takes out a sheet of paper. I stand next to him, watching him as he writes: "Eid, O Eid, you have come back anew. Remind us of old Eids or new ones preview." He looks out at the alley, thinking. I can tell that he is trying to write new lines to finish the famous poem like he does each Eid. I say: "Well, aren't we going out?" He doesn't answer. After a second, he stands up in a huff. He gets out his shaving kit and puts it on the table. I bring him a cup of water. He gets his brush wet and then rubs it on the soap.

I get my new shirt. I pull up its collar and press a stiffener into the slots for it. I put on the trousers from my new suit. The material is heavy and rough. He tells me to just wear the trousers and shirt because it is very hot. I give in, but I don't really want to. I make sure that my lucky Quran verses are rolled up in my back trouser pocket. I can hear the noise of the children in the alley. I rush to the balcony. They are all wearing their new clothes for the Eid. The girls have bows in their hair. They're shouting all in the same breath: "Open up those coin sacks, hand us our gifts back, O *halu*!" They let off firecrackers. Samir has a strip of "Italian War" brand. Its pellets hit the ground and light up.

I turn around and walk back inside. I pace back and forth for a long time until he finishes shaving. He rubs his cheeks and under his chin with an aluminum roll coated in silver foil. He leaves his razor on top of the desk. He gets up. His clothes come off. His dress shirt goes on. He buttons it. A button snaps off and falls to the ground. I pick it up. He looks around in the upper drawer of the dresser until he finds a sewing needle and some thread. He tries to get the thread through the eye of the needle but can't. He gives them to me. I wet the end of the thread in my mouth and stick it through the eye with no problem.

He puts on the trousers that go with his white suit. He fastens his suspenders. "Bring me my shoes." I bring him the brown shoes with the white tips. I clean them with a piece of cloth. He sits down on the edge of the bed and presses his feet into the shoes, then he ties their laces. He sits there for a second, staring at the floor. I hurry him up: "Come on now." He stands up and puts on the suit jacket. He takes his fez off the hat rack and puts it on. He twists each end of his moustache, turning them upward with his fingers.

He closes the two glass panes of the window, and looks around for the key in the stack of scattered clothes and covers on top of the bed. He grabs the white parasol hanging on the rack. He presses on its handle to open it. A long tear appears on one side and he throws it to the side in disgust. He reminds me not to forget my English textbook and my homework notebook.

We leave the room and lock the door. Fatima is there at the door to the storage room. "Happy holidays, Sidi. Come back safe." He gives her money for the Eid and she kisses his hand: "God preserve you, Sidi." The late night crier faces us at the end of the alley. For the first time, I see his face in the daylight. It is tanned and covered in wrinkles. He says to father: "Happy holidays, Bey," and Father gives him half a franc.

The grocery shop is closed. We make it to the square. Swings have been set up in front of the entrance to Husseiniya Street. We get on the tram at the front door next to the driver. I twist my neck to see the signs pasted overhead: "No Spitting." "Do not talk to the driver." We get off in Abbasiya Square, and get on the white tram. We get off at Ismailiya Square. Father takes a handkerchief and wipes the sweat off his face. He moves it around to the back of his neck and under his collar. He takes off the fez. He wipes off his bald spot then runs the handkerchief along the lining inside his fez. Puts the handkerchief on top of his head so its edges hang down on his forehead. He presses the fez down over it.

We go into the street and look up towards the house facing us at its end. He asks: "Do you think they're home." *The sun is scorching and he has a watermelon under each arm. He takes off his fez and wipes away the sweat on his bald head with a handkerchief. The windows of the balcony are closed. We go back without a sound; his face looks sad.*

I look hard at the wooden blinds that let you see through their narrow slats. One of them is raised just a little. I say: "If they'd gone out, they would've closed them."

We stop in front of the only grocer that is open. Boxes of dried cod for Eid are stacked up in front of it. They are wide and painted snow white. Stacks of watermelon and canta-loupe melons. Some crates of grapes and figs. Father buys one *oka* of *binati* grapes and another of *faiyyumi* figs. He chooses the figs that have just opened up and leaves the ones that are still closed. He carries them in two bags that he clutches to his chest, one in each arm. We go back to the house. There are two cars in front of it, a Skoda and a Chrysler with a bubble shaped bonnet. The front entrance is paved with colored tiles. We go up the stairs.

The noise of the Eid festival comes from the first floor. A big family is living in two connected apartments. We keep going up to the second floor. The door overlooking the balcony is closed, but the one facing the stairwell is open. We go inside. Father plops down on the couch panting. I stand next to him. He breathes in and relaxes, removing his fez and putting it on top of a pillow in the middle of the couch. A strong breeze runs from the door that opens on to the stairwell to the guest room that connects to the veranda. Shawqi comes running out. He is about my age. He is good looking with light skin and smooth black hair. He is wearing a complete new suit. It's a brownish color with white stripes that run lengthwise. His crepe-soled shoes are also brown. His sister Shareen runs out after him in a bright colored dress with short sleeves. Her hair is brushed back, parted in the middle, and tied with a bow behind her head. Her forehead has a deep mark from some sort of fall. They grab on to father. He hugs them and kisses them. He gives them their Eid money.

My sister Nabila walks in coming from the direction of the kitchen. She wears a dark red sleeveless dress. Her face is made up with powders and rouge. She kisses father on the cheek. "Happy holidays, papa." He tries to kiss her back, but she moves away. "No, papa, you'll ruin my make-up. Come on out to the veranda. There's a nice breeze there." Father waves at her to wait just a second. He says: "Seems like I have a touch of sunstroke or something."

She says: "I'll bring you some water with a drop of vinegar."

"Give me a glass of water first."

She calls out: "Khadra!" The new maid comes running. She is dark and taller than my sister. She has a big chest. Moves around quickly in her colored *gallabiya*. Her hair is tied back with a colored handkerchief that matches the *gallabiya*. Her feet look clean in her nice plastic flip-flops. She goes for the jugs on top of the tray sitting on the sideboard next to the radio. She takes the brass cover off one of them and pours water from it into a glass. She puts it on a small silver tray and offers it to father. She turns to me: "Would you like a drink, sir?" She hands me another glass. I gulp down the cold water with a touch of rosewater. Nabila tells her to bring a cup of water with a drop of vinegar.

Father takes off his suit coat. He throws it to the side. Nabila picks up the fez and coat. She hands them to me: "Hang them up inside." I'm still carrying the English textbook and the notebook in my right hand. She says: "Put them on the dining table."

I fly off to the bedroom with the fez and coat. I have to get on my tiptoes to hang the coat on one of the hooks of the coat rack. I set the fez down over it. I look up and smell something. Nabila has gathered up some mangoes from the garden and left them on the dresser. *Mother offers slices of mango on a round tray made of china with colored drawings on it. It has a metal border ringing it. I like to set it on top of the rug sometimes and use it as a square with my cars, made of match boxes, moving around it. She gives Tante Dawlet a small plate with a fork and knife. She takes a slice and puts it in front of her on the plate. I wait for my turn.*

I go back to the living room. Father is stretched out on his left side over the couch with his head resting on a white towel under his arm. The maid brings the water and vinegar. I take it from her and say that I know how to pour the drops from it. I lean over him. I press a finger into the vinegar water. I put it on his ear. I keep doing it until I hear a sizzling noise. Father turns over to the other side, switching the towel with him. I put drops in his other ear. He sits back up, keeping the towel against his ear. He says: "There, I've snapped out of it."

Uncle Fahmi joins us in his quick step with his big belly. He leans a little to the right to check how he looks in the mirror over the sideboard. A light breeze catches the folds of his white, flowing *gallabiya.* "Happy holidays, Khalil Bey! The backgammon table's ready. It's Eid today. The winner gets a riyal." Father smiles: "Just let me catch my breath." Uncle Fahmi drags one of the dining table chairs over and turns it around to face the couch. He lights a cigarette and gives me my Eid money. It's a new bill worth five piastres with a picture of King Farouk inside an oval border.

Khadra brings a tray with Eid cookies, shortbread ones and ones with powdered sugar. She puts it down on a small table in front of father. Nabila hands me a small plate. I put two cookies on it. I bite into one and find it stuffed with *melban,* a clear nougat. Father takes a shortbread cookie. He eats it with approval. He says it's just right because it melts as soon as he puts it in his mouth. Nabila says: "They're handmade. Mama's way. God rest her soul." Father says to me: "Taste one." I shake my head. She gets angry with me: "'I'm not hungry! I'm not hungry!' You'll keep saying it over and over until you shrivel up and blow away." Fahmi is smiling and looking away from her at us as he says: "Look who's talking." He picks up a powdered-sugar cookie. She turns towards him and shoots her eyes straight toward his stomach: "I guess I should just let myself look like a pregnant woman."

He ignores her and talks to father instead. "Please could you tell her to get a little fatter? I brought her some peanut brittle from Al-Hamzawi to fatten her up, but she won't go near it." Father says to her: "He's right. A man likes to have something to hang on to." They laugh. Khadra comes in with cups of coffee. Father bends over to untie his shoelaces. Khadra jumps over to help him. She brings him some cloth slippers. He asks her what village she is from and he gives her Eid money. He lifts up his left leg and stretches it out on the couch under the right one. Fahmi lights a cigarette and then leans over and lights father's too.

"Shall we play here or out on the veranda?"

Father answers: "The veranda, of course. But wait a second until my sweat is all dry."

"It's a person's right in this heat to go out in a polo shirt and shorts."

Father says that his cousin is happy to go out in a shirt with short sleeves and with no fez during the summer, like some queer.

I have a coughing fit. As she looks at me with concern, Nabila says that tuberculosis has started to spread. *She comes up to the bed I am lying in with her two children. She stands over my head. She watches me cough. Uncle Fahmi tells her that it is a normal cough and that the whooping cough has gone away. She says: "Alright, tomorrow papa is coming to take him." In the morning, I root around the nooks and crannies of the wide apartment in the pyjamas of her son Shawqi. I make sure to stay away from the covered furniture. I ask her when father is going to come. She says: "In the afternoon." At noon, she shuts the windows and the room turns dark. She gets caught up in packing bags and closing up closets as though she's going on a trip. She gets outdoor clothes ready for the children. No one speaks to me or gets clothes ready for me. I ask Shareen: "Are you going out?" She whispers: "We're going to my aunt's." "Are you taking me along?" "No. You're staying with S'aadiya until grandpa comes to get you."*

Hajj Hamdi, Uncle Fahmi's older brother, comes out and joins us. He wears a white *gallabiya* and moccasins. He has a big beard that he has trimmed carefully. White hairs have spread all through it. He is carrying silver prayer beads in his hand. He says: "Have you heard about the bombs?"

Father asks: "You mean the Benzion and Gattegno department store bombs? The Muslim Brothers are really pushing it to the limit."

Uncle Fahmi brings in the backgammon board. "Let's go to the veranda." They go into the guest room and out on to the veranda. I follow them. I stop for a second, though, at the doorway. They sit on a country-style couch with metal chairs around it. I hear the voice of Hajj Hamdi asking about Shawqi and Shareen. Uncle Fahmi's voice: "They're playing downstairs." "How did they do in the exams?" Nabila's voice: "They passed easily, thank God. Like they do every year."

Uncle Fahmi notices me. He asks: "What about you?" I go out to them and sit on the edge of the couch next to father. He cuts in and answers for me: "He has to make up English. Where is Sameera?" Uncle Fahmi says: "They're getting some sun up at Ras al-Bar. We'll catch up with them after Eid, inshallah."

Nabila says: "Papa, can you imagine that Shareen wants to wear shorts?"

Uncle Fahmi opens the backgammon set. Hajj Hamdi plays a game with father, then excuses himself and leaves. Uncle Fahmi takes his place. I have a hard time following the game. I can't believe how fast they play. They're tied after two rounds. Uncle Fahmi suggests a rubber match to decide the winner.

The maid comes in and says: "Lunch is ready." Uncle Fahmi closes the backgammon set and gets up. We head back to the dining room. He bends over and looks at himself in the mirror.

He stretches his hand out and runs it over his light hair, then straightens back up. He snatches a cookie off the tray sitting on the sideboard and devours it. He points out a long picture hanging over the mirror and asks father: "What do you think of this? Be honest. Is it better than the old one or not?"

Father heads toward his chair, but Uncle Fahmi stops him, grabbing his arm as he shoots a glance at my sister. "What do you think of my taste? The lady of the house doesn't like it." I study the picture. Its colors are dark. In its corner, there's a tiny person whose face you can't make out and he is looking at something hidden in the blur of colors. Maybe an overturned boat.

He sits at the head of the table. Nabila sits at the other end facing him. Shawqi and Shareen come in and join us. Uncle Fahmi tells the maid to light the chandelier. His eyes move quickly from plate to plate. They stop at the roasted chicken in the rectangular pan. As he stretches his hand toward the chicken, he winks and says to father: "Breast or thigh?" They exchange smiles.

He raises a thigh up to his mouth. He looks out of the corner of his eye at my sister. She is using her knife and fork. He finishes it off quickly and has another go at the rest of the chicken. She gives him a stern look. He tears off a piece and raises it to his mouth. She says: "See, papa, he eats like a *fellah*." He keeps chomping at the chicken as though he doesn't care.

We finish off with slices of watermelon. We wash our hands in the bathroom. The maid brings in a tray with glasses of Kawther cola.

Nabila asks father: "Do you want to nap inside?" He says

he prefers the couch on the veranda. She brings him a white *gallabiya* that she keeps especially for him. He takes it and goes into the guest room.

Khadra finishes taking everything back to the kitchen and cleaning off the table. Uncle Fahmi snatches a cookie with powdered sugar. He tosses it into his mouth. He asks me to sit down at the table. He sits down next to me. I open my English textbook. I read the lesson. He explains to me what the words mean. My attention is divided between his dull voice and the voices of the children in the street. He gives me an exercise to do, then goes into the bedroom. My sister follows him.

Quiet falls over the room. I start answering the questions, but I get up after a little while. I leave the dining room. I go to the country-style toilet and take a pee. I go back to the dining room. Then I step carefully over to the keyhole of the bedroom door. The bed comes into view. Fahmi is wearing white boxer shorts that go all the way to his knees. He is lying on his left side facing me. Nabila is behind him lying on her back. Her knees are up. Her bare thighs show.

I go back to my seat and stare at the picture. From outside, a familiar voice reaches my ears. "Kaymak Gelato!" An old man in a hurry pushes a handcart in front of him with metal cans of ice cream covered by cheesecloth. The sweet cream-flavored barrel is made from whole milk. The strawberry flavor has real fruit in it. He repeats his call like a braggart. I am hoping the maid will go down and buy from him, but I don't hear the door of the apartment opening up.

Father appears in the doorway of the guest room in shirt and trousers. Uncle Fahmi comes out of the master bedroom in his *gallabiya*. Nabila follows him in a blue dress. Khadra brings in some green tea. Uncle Fahmi says: "We have Lipton too." He snatches a powdered sugar cookie. We drink the tea then move to the veranda.

Khadra brings the coffee. Uncle Fahmi asks father if he is up to a new backgammon match. Nabila insists we should play a game of gin rummy instead. She shuffles and deals the cards. When I say I want to play, father scolds me. I move away to the end of the couch. I stick my finger up my nose. Nabila wins the hand. Happily, she gathers up the cards and the piastres that she has won. Her husband hides his anger by pretending to smile.

Her voice rises suddenly: "Shame on you! Get up and go wash your hands." I jump up right away without looking at anyone. I follow her to the French-style bathroom. She points to the plastic cover of the toilet. There's two footprints on it. "Are you the one that climbed up on it and left these?" I tell her I peed in the other toilet. She doesn't believe me. I wash my hands with soap. She asks me: "Does papa have money in the bank?" I say I don't know. She keeps asking questions: "Doesn't he have a checkbook?" I repeat that I don't know anything.

I follow her back to the veranda. I stop at its door. A gentle breeze is swaying the light fitting on the ceiling. In the distance, a small, weak spot of light trembles. *The dining room is dark. Its window is open. Light from the street lamp shines down on the dinner table.*

I go over to my sister's husband. I stretch out my arms holding the workbook. He takes it but puts it to the side until the hand is finished. He reviews my answers and gives it back to me. He pats my shoulder in encouragement. Father gets up. We go to the hall. I bring him his jacket and fez. My sister disappears. She comes back with a shoebox wrapped in string. She puts it on the table. We head toward the door. Nabila says: "The cookies." Father pokes me with his elbow. I go over to the box and pick it up by the string. A large, round spot from the shortening has stained its side.

We gather in the afternoon on the five steps that lead up to the house on the corner. Samir, Safwat, and a fat boy all live in the last house at the end of the alley. We play cards. Selma, Samir's sister, joins us. About my age or a bit older. She wears a sleeveless dress. Her arms are small. She sits on the landing in front of their apartment. We are down below her. She is staring with a serious look. I raise my head. She parts her legs. I notice her thighs. Her mother's voice comes out from inside the apartment. She's yelling at her husband. *I wait for my father's voice to call me, as he does every night at just the time when it starts to grow dark. I make out strange noises coming out of our house. Leaving my playmates, I run to the entrance of the house and push on the iron door. The light is on in the stairwell. I go up two steps. The apartment's door is open. My father is fully dressed and sitting in a chair under the window that faces the skylight. He is holding his fez upside down in his lap. He is frowning. Mother is going back and forth with her hair all messed up. She shouts and yells and swears. She attacks him, snatching the fez from his hand, throwing it on the ground, and stomping it hard with her feet. She snatches the reading glasses from the breast pocket of his coat. She crushes them on the tiles. My father is frozen in place. He says firm words to her: "That's enough now, Row-haya. Don't cause a scene." She runs to the window to the skylight. She opens her arms up as wide as they'll go and starts saying strange words over and over. After a while, she calms down. My father takes up the fez from the ground. He puffs out its sides again. He sets its border straight again and presses on it a couple of times. He rubs it with his hands, then puts it on. He stands up and he takes me outside.*

Siham, Selma's older sister, appears at the doorway to their apartment. She's wearing an indoor *gallabiya* without sleeves. There is a basket full of laundry on top of her head. She goes up the stairs. I watch the sway of her hips until she disappears.

Selma points to the top story of our house. She asks us if we know what happened early that morning. The police broke into the house and arrested Wadie.

I ask her: "Wadie who?"

"The son of Um Wadie."

"Why? Is he a crook?"

"No. A communist."

"What's that?"

She says she doesn't know.

"What does he look like?"

I can't remember ever seeing him. She says he is a university student who was going around to all the houses last year telling people how to prevent cholera.

The wind blows up her dress and she reaches down and pulls it over her knees. She leaves her legs far enough apart, though, that we can still see something. There is a dark space that goes up between them. I notice she is not wearing panties. *Mother stretches her hand under her gallabiya. She pulls out a big piece*

184

*of cloth that is soaked in blood. She goes to the bathroom. She comes
out after a little bit. I call her but she doesn't answer. She looks like she
is annoyed. She tilts her head and listens, like some kind of voice has
come into her head. She heads to the window. I go over to her carefully.
I lie down on the ground and look up her dress, even though I know she
is going to be mad. She is not wearing underwear. She pushes me aside.*

I put my cards together. I look at Selma. She is looking at
the ground, with a serious face. When she raises her head, our
eyes meet. She turns her eyes away. My gaze falls back on her
legs. You can see even more. *I go up to the landlord's apartment to
borrow a pinch of salt. His two girls pass me on the stairs. They ask me
in a whisper what my mother was talking about last night when she was
screaming at my father. I don't understand which time they mean. One
of them asks me with a smile: "What is this about strands of hair?" I tell
her. Their faces go red and they break into muffled laughter.*

The ululations ring out from Hakmet's house. Selma raises
her eyes to the balcony up above Safwat's house. Abdel Hamid, our landlord's crazy son, is standing there, fully dressed
and squeezing a newspaper in his right hand. He looks over
at us.

She shows all of her legs, then lets the dress fall again. She
stands straight up. She disappears into her apartment. Samir's
mother yells out his name. The voice of Safwat's mother rings
out, calling for him. They leave and the fat boy follows them.
I wait there for a second, then I sneak up the stairs to the roof.
Its door is shut. I push on it and it opens. A basket of laundry
is in the middle. Some of what was in it is hanging on the line.
There is no sign of Siham. I go over towards the room of the
engineering student. My heart is pounding. The door is shut.

I listen but I don't hear a thing. I put my eye to the keyhole. All I can see is an empty desk, but I hear movement behind the door. I run back to the door to the stairs and I go down in a hurry.

More ululating pours out of the bride's house. I go up to our apartment. Father sits in the living room. Fatima complains to him about her husband. She says he is always getting drunk on homemade liquor. After that he gets violent and beats her up. Father tells her not to make a big deal of it. He asks her to bring one of the empty cans that the aged cheese comes in. He tells her to wash it well with soap and water, then let it dry. He adds bread crumbs to water to soak them. He adds more water. He sends her to buy beer yeast from the baker. She wraps herself in her black coat and goes out. I stand on the balcony. She comes back with the yeast. Her husband Abbas meets her at our doorway. "Where've you been, bitch?" She answers back, confidently: "My boss Sidi Khalil sent me to the souq."

Father puts the yeast in the can. He stirs it. He tells her to wait three days and then give some of it to Abbas. He says the mixture is called "booza" and that it is good for the stomach and it will give him a buzz too. He says it will help him to get off the liquor. She bends over and kisses his hand: "Our Lord preserve you, Sidi."

He tells her to move the pillows to the other end of the bed so we can face the balcony and catch a bit of the breeze. I smell herring being cooked. I ask him why they don't just eat it. He says that it is the food of poor people.

I stand on the balcony. My eye is on the apartment of the bride. A pushcart comes into the alley carrying a big load of chairs and colored curtains like the ones that people use at memorials too. They are carried up to the roof of the building. Father lets me go out. I meet the children gathered around the door to the building. We go up the stairs to the roofs, then come down. The sun goes down and the mantle lamps are lit up. They test the megaphone: "Hello. Hello. One, two, three." We crowd around the table with the wedding punch. We take the chairs in the front rows and they scold us and chase us to the back. We wait anxiously. Finally, the couple appears at the entrance to the rooftop. Hekmat looks pretty in her wedding clothes. The groom is shorter than her ... fatter too. He wears a black suit and a necktie shaped like a bow. They take their seats on a platform at the end of the roof.

The belly dancer arrives. Short and dark. The drummer starts reciting jingles from the films of Shakookoo and Soraya Helmi. The dancer goes away for a second and then comes back in a dance costume. Her arms are bare. I can see the top of her chest. We clap along. She dances to the song "The Postmen Complain Because of All My Letters." She circles the wedding couple. She bends backwards as she dances. She puts her head in the groom's lap. For a second, you can see the top of her thighs. She sits in the front row to rest. One of those sitting in the front gives her a piece of cardboard to fan her head and chest and shoulders with. I sneak between the chairs to get closer to her. I stand right behind her. I reach out and touch her plump arm just below the shoulder. I am expecting it to be hot. I am surprised by its coldness.

D r. Aziz asks me: "How'd you do in the makeup exam?" Father answers: "He passed, thank God. The main thing is to not have to do it again." Everyone looks at a plump woman wearing trousers on the opposite pavement. The lights from the shops shine down on her back and make clear the roundness of her bottom. The turbaned sheikh says: "See the old lady that has no shame. Everything's showing." The priest slaps his hands together and says: "The world's gone to hell." The turbaned sheikh says: "Do you think we lost in Palestine for nothing? That was a punishment from our Lord." Refaat says: "Our cannons were blowing up in our faces." Father says: "King Abdullah was colluding with the Jews." Dr. Aziz says: "The Jewish forces expelled half a million Arabs into Transjordan, Syria, Lebanon, and Egypt and all Azzam Pasha can tell us is that they'll burn in hell for it." They laugh.

Refaat is suspicious. He says: "Was our loss in the London Olympics another punishment from God?" Abdel 'Alim says: "Thousands of pounds were thrown at our team and it all went to waste. We should give it the same name as the war, the

Olympic 'Catastrophe.' Now they're trying to say we'll start getting ready right away for the 1952 Olympics."

The sheikh offers the things he bought for the hajj: a cloth pouch for water to drink and to wash with and a wide leather belt called the *kamar* that the pilgrim wraps around his waist under his clothes to keep his money in. Father looks impressed by the new shirt that Refaat Effendi is wearing.

"Where'd you get it?"

"From Shimla for 58 piastres."

A plump, dark man comes up to us. His fez is in his hand. His hair is thick and black. He has a huge head with a big wide face. Hajj Abdel 'Alim and Refaat Effendi stand up: "Please join us, Mandour Bey." Father kicks me, so I'll get out of my chair for him. Abdel 'Alim says: "Dr. Mandour is from my same village of Minya al Qumh. He was involved in the 1919 revolution." Dr. Mandour is shy as he speaks: "Really, I was just a child then. I'd come back from school on a donkey. From on top of the Mathoubus Bridge, I saw a demonstration of effendis and fellahs together, chanting for independence and for Saad Zaghloul. The English soldiers came out of the police station and started to fire at them. That day, more than 100 were shot and many of them died. I went back to the village with the news. People gathered and grabbed their axes to go break up the government's railroad tracks, but Othman Abaza, who was a pasha and the biggest landowner in the area, caught up with them and calmed them down."

Refaat says: "Just the same, we'll consider you one of the heroes of the revolution and vote for you to represent our precinct." Dr. Mandour laughs: "That is if we even have the elections." Abdel 'Alim says to the priest: "What about you, your holiness? Who are you voting for?" The priest says: "God's truth be told, I committed to vote for Girgis Salih, the candidate of the Saadist Party." Father says: "Me too." Dr. Aziz says: "This country needs an election sweep that'll bring in a new government." Refaat says: "That's not possible as long as we have emergency law." Father says: "We need the emergency laws because of all these political assassinations and the war. If they let them expire and had elections, the Wafd party would come to power."

Dr. Mandour challenges him: "So what's wrong with that?"

"We'd go back to bribes and abuse of power."

Dr. Mandour tries to control himself: "So, you, sir, believe that right now there's no bribing and abuse of power going on?"

Abdel 'Alim says: "The doctor is right. We saw what the papers wrote about the Minya airport and the relationship between the politicians and the land owners."

Dr. Mandour keeps going: "Besides, the Wafd isn't just Othman Muharram and Fouad Serag el-Din. There are other members who are good, patriotic people. The important point is that this state we're in now won't do. Prices are going up every day. School fees are rising. The king goes to the automobile club every night and gambles. The other officials go to the *tiro* gallery to place their bets."

The turbaned sheikh asks: "What is this *tiro* thing?"

"It's betting on shooting matches at the Rifle Club."

A breeze stirs up a pile of dirt at the end of the street and it comes down on us. Abdel 'Alim says that repair workers have been digging up the streets and leaving their dirt on the sides to be stirred up by wind and traffic. Then they start to level off the street with gravel, but without paying attention to how high they go, so that the street level comes up higher than the street that meets it, so they have to start the repairs all over again to make the street level with the rest of the neighborhood, and so on and so forth. Dr. Mandour says: "It is all to the benefit of the sub-contractors. They've become millionaires with guard dogs and servants collecting salaries that university graduates can only dream of."

Refaat says: "It's gotten to where we can't even get on the bus because it's so damn packed." Dr. Aziz says that the companies being taken over by the government are losing lots of money. "Nationalization does no good." Dr. Mandour starts to get worked up: "That's what Aboud Pasha is telling people. The companies themselves are causing overcrowding. They're making the drivers and the ticket collectors let on more and more passengers. They want to grab as much money as they can before they get nationalized, and then leave nothing but pieces of scrap metal that they call buses."

I see a magazine on Abdel 'Alim's desk. I sneak inside the shop and pick it up. It is folded open to a page with an ad for the film *Passion and Vengeance,* starring Ismahan and Yusuf Wahbi. I pick up the magazine and take it outside. I show it to father: "Ismahan has a new film out." He says: "That's an old one. She made it before she died."

"When did she die?"

"Four years ago. Isn't that right, Refaat Effendi?"

Refaat crosses his legs. His black shoes are shiny in the faint light: "Yeah, that's right. Four years."

Abdel 'Alim throws in: "Still nobody knows whether she died by God's hand or somebody killed her."

Dr. Aziz says: "Of course, she was killed. Her car crashed into the water without a driver. Where did he go?"

The turbaned sheikh asks: "So who killed her?"

Father says: "The British Secret Service. She was a spy for the Germans." *She lets father out for ten minutes to go to the bathroom. She goes with him all the way to the door and waits there until he comes back out. She leads him back to the room as she watches him carefully. He tries to touch her but she says: "Don't try it. You're a German spy and you have to go to jail. Or would you rather I tell the police and make a big scene?" I sneak inside the room with him. She locks us into the room. My father makes a joke of it. He says: "It is written for me to go to prison and this one sure is better than the government jail." To the right, there is a stack of living room chairs piled on top of each other. Their bed with its brass posts stands to our left. He tells me to take the pan out and fill it up and see what happens. I knock at the door for her to open. I fill the pan, spying on her at the same time. I rush back to the room to tell him.*

Dr. Mandour says: "Queen Nazli is the one who planned the whole murder. She was jealous of her."

I become interested now that they're talking about the king's mother. Father asks: "Why?"

"Because of Ahmad Hassanein Pasha."

"What about him?"

"She was his mistress."

"Who? Ismahan?"

"Ismahan at first, then the queen."

He talks about the crisis in cinema and theatre. He says the producers made huge profits during World War II by making comedies and fluff. Then the actors started getting salaries that nobody had dreamed of. This attracted everyone and their mother into the business of film production until the standard of films started to sink, and they went all the way down to appealing to the basest instincts of the lowest common denominator. I lean over to father and whisper in his ear: "I want to see Ismahan's film." He says to me sharply: "Inshallah."

He drags the desk chair to the balcony. The alley is dark. A faint light shows in some of the windows and balconies. He grumbles about the heat. Takes off his skull cap. He tries to fan his face with it. I stand next to him. We notice Siham leaning on her elbows in the frame of their window. The engineering student is next to her. Fatima comes to us with a stalk of sugar cane in her hand. She sees where we are looking and says that Siham became pregnant by the student and that is why they rushed into a quickie marriage. Father growls at her: "What do you care?"

She is barefoot as she sits down cross-legged on the clean bare floor tiles. She peels the stick of cane and carves off a piece with her knife and offers it to father. He laughs and says he cannot chew it. She gives it to me instead. I bite it and start to chew and keep on until it is just pulp that I spit out and throw on to the plate. She stretches her legs out in front of her. She throws the second piece to the side, saying that it's too stringy.

The light from the electric lamp grows dim. She gets up to prepare the gas lamp, thinking that the electricity is going to be cut soon. He shouts at her: "Put on some slippers." She comes back with a plate full of persimmon seeds. She sits down cross-legged and her robe comes up to show her thighs. I sit in front of her on the floor. I take a few seeds. She hides her hands behind her back, then puts them in front of her in fists. She rests them on her bare thighs. I say: "Eeny Meeny, Sayyid Ameeny. Put it all, on, this, one." I point to her right fist and she pulls back her hand, laughing. My hand lands on her bare thigh. Father says: "It's chubby, isn't it?" I grab the flesh of her thigh and answer: "Chubby."

She says: "Even the *hebb al'azziz* snacks cost more. Everything's gone up." Father says Egyptians have always suffered from bad rulers and rising prices. In the days of the Mamelukes, they suffered from the rising taxes to the point where they chanted in the streets: "Hey Bardissi, why do you squeeze me? You eat off my bankruptcy!" I ask him to tell us one of his stories. He says he once went on a trip to Turkey and toured the magnificent Yildiz Palace. Its bathroom was pure marble with fancy French toilets. He felt nature's call, so he sat on one. When he was finished, he turned the tap and was surprised to feel something strange brushing against his thighs, as though it were human hands. He jumped up and found tiny streams of water running down in all different directions.

You can tell she is impressed: "They did that in the days of the caliph?"

"What do you mean *caliph*? You don't understand a thing. When Istanbul was destroyed in the earthquake and they came to pull the people up from underneath the rubble they found all the men and women clinging to each other like this." He locks the fingers from one hand into the other.

"Aren't they Muslims?"

"The real Islam was in the days of the prophet and the Rashidian Caliphate." He tells us about the prophet and his devoutness. Then about Omar Ibn Khattab and his sense of justice. Then Ali Ibn Abi Talib and his two sons.

I ask him if he participated in the revolution of 1919 and he says: "I sure did. I left the bureau where I worked with the other clerks. We climbed into a carriage and rode through the streets, chanting 'Down with British rule,' and 'Long live Saad Zaghloul.'"

Fatima asks him: "Have you seen lots of countries, Sidi?"

He says: "Not many."

"Tell us about them, Sidi."

He says: "I'll tell you, but give me the jar first." She pushes herself up and goes to get one of the three jars placed on the tray resting on top of the ledge surrounding the balcony, so they can cool. He sips from it and takes a deep breath. He tells her to make sure the other two are full. She takes one inside to fill it up. She comes back and puts it on the tray between the lemon and the cucumber.

Father sits back in his chair. He lights up his dark colored cigarette. He says: "The first time was when I went to Sudan with the army. Um Nabila, God rest her soul, came along with me. She was pregnant with Nabila too. We rented a whole house. It was hot as hell. I looked for somebody at the place to help us get our cots unfolded but there wasn't anyone around. I saw two guys wearing white, resting under a tree. They were each propped up on one elbow playing a game of tic-tac-toe. One of them was chewing on something that made his teeth as black as coal. I called out: 'Hey, you guys!' but it was like calling to the wind. I heard Um Nabila scream. I ran back and found her back against the wall. Her face was yellow and her eyes were fixed on an untied cloth bundle and a tiny bug, a scorpion with its tail in the air. I went to smash it but I missed. It ran to the wall and escaped through the window. Um Nabila threw herself into my arms. I gave her a glass of water to drink. We had to sleep inside a big mosquito net and we put cans full of water under each leg of the bed."

Fatima puts her hand on her chest and stretches her legs out: "A person would be right to never go abroad and stay at home his whole life."

"Do you think staying here was that safe?"

He tells us about the draft and how people were trying to escape being put in the army. The poor were maiming themselves to get out of it. Cutting an arm or leg or even gouging an eye. The rich were all bribing their way out of it, paying what they called "a replacement charge." Thieves and robbers started to target the people who took the payoffs.

He fans his face with his cap. "I was sleeping with a revolver under my pillow. That and an envelope full of money. At night I woke up once to the sound of steps on the roof. I took the revolver out and got up really slowly. I stood in the dark and then yelled out strong and bold: 'Who's there?' No one answered. Fifteen minutes passed and no sound. After a while, I heard the dawn call to prayer and went back to sleep."

Fatima looks at him amazed: "Oh my. You have a heart of steel, Sidi." He goes on, saying that being on the road wasn't safe either. Especially in the south. At night, gangs would gather along the side of the road, coming back from a soirée at the house of some police chief or local official. The night would be black like kohl. His hand held his money belt real tight and his eyes darted around in the dark. "My eyesight was 20/20 back then. Once I was hit by a bullet." He points to a scar on his forehead, just between his eyes. "Once I was stabbed with a switchblade." He turns his head so we can see another scar on the nape of his neck.

I ask: "Do you still have the revolver?"

"No. The English were collecting all firearms, so I hid it in the garden of the villa. Probably, Nabila's uncle who was living with us stole it and sold it."

Silence echoes around us. After a little while, he says: "The important thing is that one's got to know how to act. Once I was riding the tram. Two guys got on. One stood on the stairs to the right and the other jumped off to the left. He asked me what time it was. I suspected they were pickpockets. I reached into my pocket and pulled out a closed hand. I pretended to look at it and told him it's about such and such. The guy on the right burst out laughing and said: 'Leave him alone, champ. It's clear he's just like us.'"

Fatima laughs and slaps her hand on her bare thighs. I ask him to tell us about Hafiz Naguib. He says that he was a sly thief and an international crook. He became famous for his ability to disguise himself and escape from the police. "Once they caught him in the disguise of an Italian baron, another time as the Turkish ambassador. A third time he was dressed like a priest. Another time he was standing in a cage in the courtroom. He stood up to hear his sentence. The judge turned for a second, then he couldn't find him. Up until today, still no one knows how he escaped from the cage."

She says: "By the prophet, Sidi, please please tell us one of Juha's tales." He says that once upon a time Juha was living in a house. After a couple days, he started complaining to the landlord about a rumbling sound coming from the ceiling that made him afraid it was going to come crashing down. The landlord reassured him by saying that by the grace of God the ceiling was sound, so Juha says: "That's exactly what I'm afraid of." "Why?" he asks. He answers back: "I don't want God's grace to rain down upon us." Father bursts out laughing until tears flow down his cheeks and he starts to wipe them away, saying: "May our Lord keep us safe." I ask him why he says this and he tells me that happy times are always followed by bad ones. *We have our breakfast on a boat off Rod el Farag Isle in the Nile. Ful beans and heavy cream with honey. The wooden table is painted blue. Mother is humming a tune. We get off the boat and we walk through a farm. We go into a fruit orchard. My father buys bananas and dates. The owner of the fruit stand invites me to eat guava. I eat until I'm stuffed. We leave the fruit stand. I trip on a drain cover. I fall down and hit my head on it. I throw up all that I've eaten.*

Abdel Wahab's voice wafts in from Um Zakiya's radio. He sings: "In the sea I did not desert you/ On land, you abandoned me/ For gold I could never sell you/ You sold me for straw." Father sings along: "I was a flower in a garden/ You plucked me/I was a candle burning in a hearth/ You smothered me." He shakes his head sadly and says: "Once you were 'Mr. Khalil,' like a flower in people's hands that they'd sniff, then you turned into something else, like the old rotten leftovers to be tossed out." Fatima says: "Please don't talk that way, Sidi. Look at you, fresh as a rose."

He gets up and walks across the room. His eyes are on her bare thighs. Abbas's voice is calling her. She covers her legs quickly and jumps up. She says: "Good night, all." He goes with me to the bathroom to get ready for bed. He turns off the light. He lies down beside me. He leaves the door to the balcony open. I say to him: "Aren't you scared a robber will come in?" He says: "Whosoever depends on God, He protects." He recites the verse of the throne. I think about the angels protecting us, flapping their wings around us. I fall asleep.

Suddenly, I am awakened by moving around next to me. Father's scratching between his legs. I sleep. I wake up again. He's still scratching. His hand's moving faster. He's panting. He turns toward me. I close my eyes and fall deep into sleep.

Chapter Four

The strike starts right after the first class. We repeat the chant of a student, wearing a fez, from fifth grade. "Long live Egypt, Free and Independent!" We call for more armed opposition to Zionism and for the English to quit Egypt and for the unification of Egypt and Sudan. We leave the school grounds. Some suggest that we go to the university to join up with the students there, others that we go the other way towards Fuad the First School and Al-Husseiniya School. I remember father's instructions. I pull myself out of the group and steal away, across the side streets that lead towards our house.

He opens the door for me wearing his flannel *gallabiya*. His white skull cap covers his head. A frown. The leftovers from breakfast are on the table in the hall. I tell him the story of what happened. He says: "Put down your satchel, sit down, and study." Our room is all gloomy and the bed has not been made. I ask: "Did Fatima not show up or something?" He gives a short answer: "No. Put the satchel down on the desk." I take out the history textbook. I open to the chapter about the Islamic Empire in the age of Othman. I read the story of his dispute with Ali Ibn Abi Talib and the way it ended in tragedy for both.

The doorbell rings. I run to open it. Fatima is carrying a bundle of clothes. She is wearing flimsy plastic sandals. Tears stream down her cheeks. She says Abbas beat her and kicked her out, and that she is heading back to her village. Father says to her: "Calm down. Have a seat." She says she cannot spend another night with Abbas. Father says our house is her house and that she can stay on with us until Hajj Abdel 'Alim gets out of jail. "Come on, don't cry so much. Get up and get to work."

She cleans the table, the room, and the kitchen. He tells her to get a bath ready for herself. She brings the stove into the living room. She lights it and puts a pot of water over the flame. She fills the zinc basin about half way up with water. She puts it in the middle of the room. We follow her in. He tells her to wash her hair well and asks: "Do you have a comb?"

"Yes, why?"

"For lice."

She says her hair is clean.

"Do you have a loofah or should I bring you ours?"

She says: "No. I have one."

"Do you have clean clothes?"

"I have some."

He tells her to put her dirty clothes to the side to be washed later. We leave the room and she closes the door behind us.

We go into our room. I sit at my desk and start studying again. Father lights a cigarette. He leaves the room. I follow.

"Papa, why do they say about our master Ali, 'God be generous to his face'?"

"Because he never looked upon the nakedness of any human … even himself."

I ask: "Is that a sin?"

"Yeah." *Selma bares her legs. There is a dark space between them. Mama Tahiya moves to her other underarm. She turns her head to study it. She feels it with her fingers. She stands up. She tells me as she gently takes hold of my ear: "Get to your room. Sit there and don't leave." I take her hand pleading, "Please, I'm begging you Mama, not by myself." She studies me with a smile. "Okay. You can sit in the living room, but only on the condition that you don't spy on me."*

I go into our room and then come back out. He walks around the living room, going back and forth with his hands clutched behind his back. He tells me she is a simpleton who could burn herself. Or she could trick us and not really take a bath: "Take a look and see what she's doing." I peek through the keyhole. My glasses knock against the door. I press them back up on my nose. I start looking again. I see her sitting down in the tub without anything appearing but her bare shoulders. Steam comes up from the pan of water. *Mother grabs hold of the metal jar. She fills it half way with hot water. She forgets to mix in a little bit of cold.*

I tell him she is naked and sitting in the tub. He says: "Let's see," and he bends over to look through the keyhole. He stands back up and walks around the dining table. He rubs his moustache with his finger. I notice that his eyes are shiny. He tells me to offer to help her rub her back. I do it without wanting to. She turns me down. She walks out after a while wearing a colored *gallabiya* and combing her hair. Water drips off it. He asks her if she boiled her clothes and she says: "Yes."

She changes the water in the basin. She brings in the wash-tub for laundry from the kitchen. She puts it next to the basin. Father paces in the living room while he watches her. I get out my history textbook and I sit at the table, facing the guest room. She sits down on top of the low, wooden kitchen stool. She gathers up her *gallabiya* between her legs and her knees are bared and even part of her thighs. *She is bending over her folded right leg. She puts a piece of the halva putty on top of her foot. She lifts it off and then rubs on it. She puts it on the middle of her leg. She does the same thing over again up closer to her thigh.*

She moves clothes from the basin to the tub and rubs them. She dunks them in the water in the basin. She rubs them some more then wrings them out and hangs them to dry on the clothesline hanging in the skylight. She uses up all the water in the basin and the sink and then dries the floor. She takes the burner back to the kitchen. He tells her to soak the tablecloth for a while in the tub. We can see that the top of our wooden table has a large grease stain on it.

He tells her to light the stove to heat up the food for lunch. He throws himself into cooking the piece of meat. He adds bits of charcoal to it. He gets the green salad ready. He calls me and tells me to bring in a pack of salt from on top of the sideboard. I run over to it. I stretch out my hand to take the salt. Fatima beats me to it and I pull my hand back. She calls out: "Yes, Sidi. Right away." She brings him the salt. I follow, feeling mad.

He finishes browning the meat and starts to heat up the bread over the fire. She puts two plates on the table. He says that the table is so dirty that he doesn't feel like eating. She rushes to clean it with the kitchen loofah. He asks her to wait until we have finished eating. He takes the pan of meat into our room. He puts it on the round table. She brings in the two plates and the bread. She hangs on to her own plate. He sits on the edge of the bed. I drag the desk chair over and sit in front of him. He dishes out our food first. She holds her plate out to him. He serves her. She goes to sit on the floor, so he says to her: "Sit up on the bed. You're just like my daughter." She sits next to me. I lose my appetite.

The doorbell rings. She starts to get up to open it but he signals to her to stay put. He waves at me to go and see who it is. I open the door and find Abbas in front of me.

"Is Fatima here?" I don't know how to answer.

"Okay then, can you just call the bey?"

I leave him and run in to get father. He gets up and leaves the room. He closes the door behind him. I think about following him, but I don't want to leave Fatima by herself. I stand up behind the door. She stands next to me. We listen. My father's voice: "Sit down, Abbas." His voice sounds very firm. We cannot pick up anything from the conversation. Abbas's voice makes him sound in a bad way. Father calls to Fatima. She goes into the living room and I follow. He says to her: "It's settled, my girl. Go back to your husband. He won't raise his hand again. You can come and get your clothes later, after they've dried." Abbas heads for the front door with her right behind him.

He grabs his fez with his left hand. He lifts it up, level to his chest. Bends his right arm. His right hand comes up to the fez. He brushes off its sides with his sleeve. He sets it on top of his head. Locks the door to our room. He tells Fatima to cook the spinach just the way he taught her to, and to remember to throw in a few dried chickpeas. We go out and head for the street. The grocery shop is closed. I lean over towards the chemist. He pulls me sharply by my arm. We cross to the other pavement and pass in front of Hajj Mishaal's shop. He is sitting inside. His body is huge. He is wearing a long-sleeved shirt and trousers. His hair is slicked down with Vaseline. He smiles an unsettled smile when he sees us. Father ignores him.

We turn into the next alley. We come out in the next street along. "Khalil." I turn around angrily at whoever is calling my father without giving him the title of "Bey." Aly Safa comes up to us in a rush. He is walking with his feet flying out to each side of him. He is wearing a blue suit coat and grey trousers. Father stops to let him catch up with us. They shake hands. I stand between them. Father pushes me to the right and we keep walking so that Aly Safa falls in to his left. Father asks

him: "Where've you been? Did you get married or something?"
Aly Safa says: "Do I look crazy?"

He reaches out to pat me on the cheek and asks: "Don't you have school today?" Father pushes me away from his hand gruffly and says: "These days there's a strike almost every day." Aly Safa says he is running off to the electric utilities office and he goes on ahead of us. I ask father why he pushed me to the side. He says: "The thing is, he corrupts young boys." I think about this strange puzzle.

We turn into a small side alley. There is a smell of mold and mildew. We go into a house with no doorman. We go up the steps to the second story. He knocks on the door of an apartment. A woman's voice comes out after a while: "Who is it?" Father says: "Aziza, it's me."

The voice repeats: "Who?"

"Aziza, it's me, Khalil. Open up."

"Just a minute, Bey."

The door opens to the figure of Hajj Abdel 'Alim's wife. She is taller than father and has a face that is white and beautiful with tiny black moles scattered over it. The hair on her head is wrapped in a scarf that starts at the middle of her head and goes down to her neck. There is a pigtail coming out from under it. She is carrying a child in her arms.

"Please, come in, Bey"—(she pronounces the title like all the *fellah* women do)—"You're one of the family."

Father and I go in. It is a wide hall with no furniture at all. There is a room in front of us where Sofia, the sister-in-law of the hajj is standing. Behind her you can see a bed, raised on high brass posts. Father speaks to her: "Good health to you."

She answers coldly: "Good health to you too." He ignores her tone and follows Aziza to another room. We stop at the door. The same kind of bed is there with a child lying on top of it. Father says: "I've just come to check on you. Do you want to send him food or anything?"

"The Lord preserve you, Bey. Selim has taken him food and money."

Father turns back towards the front door and I follow. "Inshallah he'll come out today. Anyway, if there's anything you need, tell me."

"May the Lord always keep you in our lives, Bey."

We leave the apartment. We go out to the main street. We head toward the closest tram stop. We get on. We change cars at 'Ataba Square. We take the new one to Abdel Aziz Street by the big fire station. The tram turns around in front of the Omar Effendi department store. We get off after two more stops. We cross the tracks to the pavement across the street. We stop in front of a huge building with crowds of people gathered in front of it. Father puts his hand on his chest right over his heart. I ask him: "What's wrong?" He says: "There are lots of pickpockets around here." We go up a few steps that pass through stone pillars. We walk into a large hallway full of people. A vendor is sitting cross-legged at the base of a marble pillar. In front of him is a tray with falafel patties, loaves of pita, and small plates of salad. He is surrounded by people eating.

At the next column is a cross-legged man with many women around him, squatting on the ground hugging their knees. He wears a *gallabiya* decorated down the front with black thread. An old fez sits on his head. A student's satchel made of canvas sits in front of him with papers stacked up on it. He has an fountain pen in his hand. We go up the steps to the second floor. We cut through the crowd until we're in a hallway with large rooms that are closed up on either side of us. Father goes up to each door and reads the paper sign nailed to it. We go on searching but it is no use, so we go back to the stairs. We're surprised by a woman pulling off her cloak, followed by her black *gallabiya*. Underneath she is wearing a man's shirt and yellow trousers from army salvage. She pulls a bench up from under the people sitting on it and uses it to attack people standing around her. A man in a *gallabiya* and skull cap tries to stop her, but she knocks him back with a head butt. We run down the steps and stop near the entrance to the building.

Dr. Mandour shows up wearing black trousers and a grey coat. He says: "Is everything alright?" An assistant comes up to him carrying his black lawyer's robe. Father says: "We read your article in the *Wafd al Misri* newspaper. What happened between you and *Akhbar al Youm?*" He laughs: "Nothing. I called it a piece of yellow journalism because it's a British publication that set out to make the case for the king against the Wafd Party. It's always calling him the just ruler, the great governor, or the leader of the faithful."

I sneak over behind the writer. A squatting woman dictates in front of him as he writes. The pen must not be absorbing any ink because he keeps dipping it into the ink bottle after every few words. He scolds her every now and then. After the writing is done, he waves for her to go over to his co-worker, who holds up a small piece of brass shaped like a ring. The woman leans over and hands him the paper. He shouts at her: "Your name?"

She answers: "Aida."

He says: "Give your complete name, woman."

"What do you mean?"

"I mean your name, followed by your father's name and your grandfather's name."

She takes out a paper rolled up in her chest and gives it to him. He unwraps it in a hurry and reads. He scratches her name into the piece of brass. The writer takes it and presses it into a small box. He studies the stamp, and asks: "Are you Aida Girguis Estafanous?" She answers with a southern accent: "Yes." He presses the stamp down on the paper and hands it to her. She gives him money. He says to her: "Give it to the head clerk." He points to the man standing nearby. His fez is taller than everyone else's and his reading glasses have dark lenses. He takes the paper from her and goes with her to the falafel vendor. She buys him a loaf of bread and a few pieces.

I hear father's voice calling my name, so I run over to him. He shouts at me for leaving him alone. We head over to the other side of the building. There is a pack of country women sitting on the ground with their children. We go into a big, crowded room. *She sits in the front row next to my grandma. She wears a black silk coat and she has a sheer grey scarf wrapped around her head. She is taller and wider than she was the last time I saw her. Grandma looks over her shoulder, worried. A strange smile is painted on her face. She looks at me without blinking. Her pale brown face is surrounded by a faded, off-white scarf. Mother notices me. I can't tell if she knows me or not. She suddenly talks to me in a very normal voice, like we've never even been separated: "How are you?" She doesn't ask me to sit next to her. She turns back to pay attention to the judge. She listens to a sheikh in a caftan and turban wearing reading glasses. I turn around looking for my father. He waves to me from the entrance to the hall. I go to him.*

We squeeze ourselves on to the end of the bench pushing over the others sitting there. We notice Selim sitting up in the front row. The judge's stand is up at the front. Lawyers gather in front of him, including Dr. Mandour in his black coat. They're talking to each other, but we can't hear them. Hajj Abdel 'Alim is standing behind iron bars. The judge says something that makes the lawyers all stand back. The clerk calls out for the other accused people to come in. All of a sudden, the hearing ends and the judge disappears through a door behind the judge's stand, followed by his helpers. The people sitting down get up and walk over to the cage holding the accused. The prisoners start calling out to their friends and relatives. Hajj Abdel 'Alim notices us. He seems very happy and not scared.

We leave the courtroom and head out to the right. After a short walk, the Abbadin Palace comes into view. Alongside I can see the wide square stretching out in front of it. *We stand in rows from the early morning all the way through to the afternoon. The school official is leading us. We're wearing the blue shirts that they've passed out to us. They look like nursery school uniforms. We wait for the appearance of the king to celebrate him on the anniversary of his coronation.*

We turn to the left and go down a street with lots of shady trees. We stop in front of a fancy building. A Nubian doorman meets us. We get into a clean elevator. It goes up slowly without making a sound. I sit down on a seat fastened to the wall. We stop at the fifth floor. We knock on the door of Tante Zeinab's apartment. Her black maid Zahra opens the door for us. She welcomes us and pulls me to her chest. She kisses my cheek. I know her whole story from father. She was owned by Tante Zeinab's family before the Khedive Ismail outlawed slavery, but she had no idea who her family was or where she had come from, so she stayed on to work for Tante Zeinab.

We sit down in a cozy sitting room by the front door. Family pictures hang on the wall. Tante Zeinab shows up after a while. She moves slowly. Dark and short. She pants the whole time because she has a weak heart. "How are you, my brother?" I know she is my father's cousin from his mother's side. And that she was engaged to him when he was young, before he married Um Nabila. She never got married after that, and she lives with her brother Shams, who also has never married, even though he is very old too. She looks at me, smiling gently. Zahra sits at her feet. Father asks: "How's your health?" She says: "Fine. All that God brings is fine. Any news of Rowhaya?"

"None." *The iron door is closed. In front of it are neighborhood women and their children. They are looking through a big crack in the coated glass. I can see mother through it, standing in front of the door to the apartment. Grandma is beside her ... and the daughters of the landlord. My father is all dressed up. His head is bare. She is screaming: "You want to poison me? You've put poison in here." She points at a glass cup sitting on the banister. Father says in a quiet and tired voice: "Relax. Drink up and it'll calm you."*

She says as she pants for breath: "Have you had lunch, my brother? We just ate and Shams has gone for a nap." She makes a big effort to get up. We follow her inside. An untidy room with no furniture in it except a round table with chairs. We sit around it. Zahra brings us spaghetti and green salad. She serves me. She sprinkles grated Egyptian Romano cheese on my plate. I try to use the fork. It is the first time I've eaten pasta with cheese. I don't finish all of it. Tante Zeinab asks her to open a jar of fruit compote. She brings in a stained glass jar and serves me pieces of apple and pear. She adds a spoon of syrup.

I go to the bathroom with father. Some machine is hanging on the wall. There is a drawing of a flame on it with the words "Shell Gas" above it. Father says it is to heat the water. We go back to the room at the entrance. Zahra brings a cup of coffee for father. He asks Tante Zeinab how much the water heater costs. She says: "Sixteen pounds." They ask each other questions about members of the family.

"Do you see Nabila, my brother?"

"Yes."

"How's she doing?"

"Well . . ." He stops and looks at me. He tells Zahra to take me to the balcony. I go along with her even though I don't want to. I steal a glance behind me. Father is talking in a low voice. He looks like he is saying something really serious. We go out on to the small circular balcony. From its left hand corner, I can see the wide, empty square in front of the palace. *He carries me in his arms and sets me down on the iron fence. His strong hand rests on my knees. I look out at the crowds gathered in the square.*

I draw a map showing the ground levels on the African con-
tinent. I mark the high ground and the low spots. I mark
off arrows showing the directions of the winds. Suddenly, a
shout goes up from the alley. I run to the balcony. The alley is
dark. The shouting is coming from the apartment of Siham
and Selma. I turn my head to look at the entrance to the alley.
I am waiting for father to come back from visiting Hajj Abdel
'Alim to congratulate him on being let out of jail. I turn around
and go back inside. I get right up to the door to our room. I
listen. The light in the living room is on. I can hear the sound
of Fatima in front of the sink. She cleans the glass of the gas
lantern. She hangs it on a nail over the sink and then disappears into the kitchen. I go out into the hall. I carefully go up
close to the door to the washroom. I can hear her lighting the
kerosene lamp.

I go back to the room. The light goes out suddenly. I call to
her. She answers. Her voice is coming closer. She says the box of
matches is empty. She tells me to look around for another one.

"Where?"

"In your room. Check the pockets in your papa's robe."

I feel my way in the dark towards the clothes stand. I stretch my hand into the pocket of the robe. I call out: "Nothing." She yells back: "Bring a sheet of newspaper." I try to remember where some newspaper might be. I tear off a page from the back of the geography notebook.

I shout: "Here's the paper."

"Give it here."

"No. Come here and get it."

"I can't see because of this dark."

I can smell in her voice that she's scared. "Neither can I."

I go up close to the door of the room. As I step into the hall, I am scared to death: "Here I am." I bump into her. She snatches the paper from my hand. *Um Ibrahim is sitting on the floor in the middle of the hall in front of the oil burner. Her hair is uncovered. It's curly and red, all washed with henna. The color of her eyes is more like grey ash. You can see that she is scared. Mother is sitting in front of her on a chair. She orders her to boil the cucumbers. Um Ibrahim looks shocked: "Boil them? Do you boil cucumbers, madam?" Mother shouts at her: "What do you care? Just do as I tell you." "Yes, madam. Of course. Just don't scream please, madam." She throws the cucumbers into the pot that sits on the fire. I am carrying a cup of coffee in my hand. Mother gets up. She takes a key from her breast pocket. She unlocks the door to our room. I carry in the cup of coffee carefully. My father takes it. I tell him what just happened with Um Ibrahim. He laughs: "Serves her right. She's been driving me crazy."*

I follow her to the hallway. I turn my face away from the doorway to the toilet. She goes ahead of me into the kitchen and then comes back with the stove. It is giving out a little bit of light. She sets it on the floor under the sink. She unhooks the oil lamp from its nail. She opens its window. She uses the stove to light the paper, and lights the lamp's wick. She gives me the lamp, saying: "Come with me to the kitchen." I say: "It's better to stay here in the hall." She says: "I have washing to do." I carry the lamp and follow her into kitchen but don't really want to. She puts the stove down on the floor next to the tub full of dirty clothes. She takes the lamp from me and hangs it on the nail on the wall. She puts the pan of water on the fire. Sits down in front of the tub on the wooden foot stool. She reaches over. Tips out a bucket of mop water. She spreads it around with her foot between the tub and the door. She waves at me to sit down on a seat that's facing her, between her and the door.

"Do you think papa's going to be late?"

She answers with a scowl: "He'll be back any minute."

The steam comes up from the pan of water. She throws the clothes into it. She stirs them around with the end of a metal ladle. She takes out one thing. Throws it into the tub. As she rubs soap over it, she shouts out from its heat.

A burst of wind rushes in from the window. The flame in the oil lamp flickers. The shadows dance on the wall. I follow them anxiously. My eyes go to a huge cockroach. It is fixed on the wall. The head is pointed at me. Its whiskers are shaking. I look up at the tub. The clothes are still piled up in it. I feel sleepy. The strong, striking smell of the toilet comes to me. She wrings out the clothes as she studies the darkness behind me in fear. I fight off the urge to turn around and look. *The ghoul shows itself, coming from far away. A huge swirl of hair spun around by the wind. The ghoul sniffs a scent of Hassan the Brave then says: "The smell of human, not like our smell or the smell of our clan!"*

The children in the alley repeat the call for the prayer of the Big Feast: "To God the Supreme be acclaim/ All praise to His great holy name." Father takes the scissors and sits me down between his knees. He gives me a haircut. I have the mirror with the cracked metal frame in my hand. I tell him the right side is higher than the left. He throws the scissors on to the desk and pushes me away from him.

"No. It's fine." *The barber unrolls the leather strip hanging next to the door of the shop. He runs the edge of the blade over it as hard as he can. He finishes shaving the customer's beard. My turn comes. He spits into the iron spittoon. I sit in the barber's chair and he ties a towel around my neck.*

I put on my suit. I look around the desktop for the notebook of songs. My hand hits the bottle of ink and spills it on to the front of my jacket and my trousers.

Father blows up: "You clumsy ... You're completely worthless. Take off your clothes."

I take off my jacket and trousers. He gets mad and pulls them off me. He examines the ink spot. I follow him to the kitchen. He sprinkles salt over it. He comes back to the hall and takes a lemon off the fruit tray. He cuts it up with a knife and squeezes one of the wedges over the salt. We go back to the room. He studies the spot in the light. He puts the jacket and trousers over the back of the chair.

He says: "It won't come clean right now. Put on your light pyjamas."

I am surprised and ask: "You mean go out in them?"

"What else can we do? I'll iron them for you and they'll look great. Pass the iron."

I drag the heavy metal iron from under the bed. He takes it to the kitchen to heat it up. He brings it back in with a wet towel. He folds the pyjama top over the bed. He covers it with the towel and passes the hot iron over it. He goes to the sleeves, then to the back. He gives it to me then irons the trousers. Grumbling, I put them on.

He prays the midday prayer then puts on his brown suit. We leave the house. We head toward the main street. A wide poster congratulates Mishaal on his return from the hajj. "May your hajj bring forgiveness and acceptance from God." We take the tram. Abbasiya, then Heliopolis. We pass in front of a fancy villa. A crowd of country women has gathered in front of it. Father says they're poor women, waiting to receive their portion of the *zakat,* the rich man's tithe of meat slaughtered for the holiday. It may be the first time they have tasted meat.

Nabila greets us by saying: "Why are you so late? Lunch has been ready for a while now." She turns to me: "Who gave you that haircut?"

Father says: "I did."

"Couldn't you've taken him to the barber?" She feels the

hair on my head. "Your hair is all curly like your mother's." She looks over my clothes. She starts to say something then keeps quiet. *Mother opens the glass pane in the front door to see who is there. She says to Nabila: "What do you want?" "To see papa." Mother tells her: "He's not your father and he doesn't know you." She slams the glass shut. I run to the room. I push the door open. Mother forgot to lock it. I go in and tell my father what happened. He steps back from the window. Nabila passes underneath it. She raises her eyes. A strange smile is on her lips.*

Showqi and Shareen come to father so he can hug them. Their clothes are new. Shareen looks over my clothes: "Oh my gosh. Are you wearing pyjamas?" Uncle Fahmi throws her a harsh look and she shuts up.

We wash our hands and sit around the table. Nabila serves us beef bouillon out of a large soup dish. Meat pastries, stewed lamb meat, and okra. Father slurps the soup loudly. My sister watches me until she catches me making a slurping sound too, then she scolds me.

After eating, we fall in along the couch in the living room. Showqi asks his father if he can go out and play with the children in the street. Uncle Fahmi tells me: "Go with him." I bend my head down and look at my pyjamas. "I don't feel like it."

Tante Samira, Uncle Fahmi's sister, shows up at the door. Her husband and her daughter Nadeen have come with her. Father uncrosses his legs and welcomes them. He studies Samira carefully. Tall and wide, like her brother. Her face is round and white and beautiful. Her big eyes are laced with kohl. Her mouth is tiny and reddened with lipstick. The smell of her perfume drifts off her clothes and spreads through the room. She wears a dark black jacket, a blouse with a high collar that comes up over the jacket collar, a full, orange skirt with pleats, and white and black shoes with high heels. Khadra brings in the chairs from the dining room, so everyone can sit.

Her husband is a clerk in the finance ministry. He wears a fez. His suit is beige. He undoes the buttons of his jacket and a big pot-belly hanging over his waist pops out.

Nadeen is seven years older than me. She has full lips, narrow eyes, and a small chest. She wears a silk dress with a tiny collar and baggy sleeves that narrow down into tight wrists. Her blouse has baggy folds around the chest and shiny buttons.

My sister seems in love with the blouse: "Oh, your little chemise is divine." She drops her eyes down over the blue skirt that hangs just above the tops of her feet by a few inches. Then down to the shoes with fat high heels: "What's that? What's that?"

Samira laughs: "It's the latest style, madam."

"Where'd you get them?"

"From Chicurel. Three days before it was blown up. You can still get them at Chemla or Oureeko."

"Nowadays, one gets scared to even go to these stores."

"Try the Egyptian Factories Outlet store."

Her husband says the time has come for the government to ban the Muslim Brotherhood. Samira complains that Nadeen wants a new hairdo in the latest style. "Two wavy tresses, a short bob around the sides, stacked up behind the neck in the shape of a beret." She crosses her legs. Her skirt comes up to her knees. She is wearing nylon stockings. Father looks over the bare part of her plump legs.

Nabila says: "Have you seen the bonnets they're coming out with now?"

Samira says that one of her husband's relatives attended a high tea organized by Princess Faiza for the new society for the welfare of women. She said she saw women in strange bonnets with large bird feathers sticking out of them. "Most of them wore black, as though they were at a funeral or something." Nabila says that black is still in style.

Father asks Nadeen what department she'll be joining the coming year. She says: "Philosophy." He suggests she start reading up on it now. He gives her the name of a book on Islamic philosophy and another in human psychology. I get the feeling that she doesn't think much of his suggestions.

A relative of Uncle Fahmi joins us. He's a student in the last year of law school. He is wearing a navy blue jacket with two rows of buttons down the front. A thin necktie. Glasses with big square frames. He uses an old-fashioned title, "aneeshta," instead of "uncle" when he talks to father. His sister Selwa, a student at the American School for Girls, comes in after him.

The two children pull back and disappear into the room of Showqi and Shareen. Alwy, the older son of Hajj Hamdy, comes in. A white coat with one button to the side and long lapels that end up at his belly button. Grey trousers with pleats and white shoes. He takes off his fez to reveal shiny, short hair that clings to his scalp.

Father asks him about his dad who is going on hajj for a second time. He says: "He should be on top of Mount Arafat right about now." Khadra brings in cups of coffee and glasses of Spathis fizzy drink.

Alwy removes a small cup made of glass from his pocket. Uncle Fahmi claps: "That's it. He brought the goods." Alwy says: "So you won't have any excuses." I know that he sets the dice before he throws them with his hand, so no one wants to throw dice with him unless they use a cup.

Everyone heads out to the veranda. Nabila puts on a sweater, saying that it's getting a bit cold. Father's cackles echo loudly. I go up to the children's room. The door's cracked open. I steal a peek. Shareen is leaning over the bed flipping through a magazine. I hear Selwa's voice saying softly that she got hold of a novel by Yusuf al-Sabaey. Shareen shows them a page from the magazine about a new American game called the hula hoop. Nadeen comes into my view. She puts her hand on her small chest. She turns toward the door but I jump back quickly. I hear her say that the Americans invented a new bra that snaps and unsnaps in the front so a girl doesn't have to reach her hand behind her back to take it off. Their laughing sounds like they're embarrassed.

I push open the door and go in. No one turns to me. Shareen flips the pages of the magazine. In a loud voice she calls out the names of the films that are playing: "*Fame or Riches,* with Mohamed Abdel Motalleb and Hassan Fayek. *The Island Princess* with Tahia Karioka, Bishara Wakeem, Ismail Yaseen, and Shakookoo. *The Man Who Doesn't Sleep,* at the Metro with Yusuf Wahbi and Mediha Yosri. *Toward Glory,* directed by and starring Hussain Sidqi. He's a bore." She throws the magazine away. I pick it up and flip through its pages. A picture of the king in military uniform wearing field glasses stares up at me. Under the picture in a fancy script, it says: "The first of the fighters."

226

I leave the room and go from there to the outer parlor. I listen next to the wall that separates it from the kitchen. The sound of dishes being washed. The door to the terrace room is closed. I pass through the hall that goes to the country-style bathroom. There's an open window facing the street. The pop of firecrackers blows through it. I get up on my tip-toes. I spot Showqi with a hunting rifle in his hand. I go into the country-style bathroom. I pee. I walk out. Open the door to the terrace room. I go in and close the door behind me. The brass handle of the dresser is broken. I pull on it. The drawers are empty. A few of them have some old clothes. I want to leave, but I hear the sound of someone running. Softly, I open the door a crack. Khadra is pushing on the door to the living room. Her face shows that she's scared. Uncle Fahmi comes from the kitchen and pushes behind her. His Mantouvli slippers slap against the tiled floor. He tries to grab her. She goes into the dining room with him behind her. I go out to the parlor. I peek through the door to the dining room. My glasses bang against the wooden door handle. He throws her down on to the couch. His face is red, his eyes flashing. He reaches his hand to her chest. She pushes him away and begs in a low voice: "Please, no, sir. Please don't cut me off." She goes around the table then passes in front of the children's room. She comes over to the door leading to the outer parlor. I jump back in a hurry. I go to hide on the terrace. I hear her open the door to the apartment and go out. I walk out of the terrace into the living room. Uncle Fahmi is bent over the mirror of the sideboard. He looks over his face. He sets his hair. He stands up straight. He goes into the guest room on his way to the veranda. The sound of his footsteps fades as he steps on to the thick carpet.

The knocking on the front door goes on. I climb over father's sleeping body and come back down on the other side. I put on my slippers, and go out to the living room. I turn the key in the door. Fatima pushes it so that it almost hits me in the face. She goes ahead of me into our room.

"You two are still sleeping?"

Father pulls up the covers as he answers: "It's Friday today."

"Come on. I'll make you breakfast."

Father falls back on his right side. His *gallabiya* comes up and shows his bare legs. My eye falls on his prick sticking out of the opening in his underpants. Blown up, like a cat's head. He stays stretched out on his side without bothering to cover himself. He looks at Fatima. He stretches out his hand and rubs his prick. He pushes up to a sitting position with his legs dangling from the side of the bed.

She asks: "What would you like to have for breakfast? Should I make hot cereal with milk or *ful* beans?" I say: "Tahini with honey." She says: "There isn't any."

Father says to me: "Here. Take a half a franc and go get some from the oil shop."

"Why don't you ask her?"

He says: "It's Friday and Abbas will want his breakfast."

She says: "Yeah, I have to go to him or he'll skin me alive."

I go to the bathroom. I get past my fears and go into the toilet room. I pee, then wash my hands and face. I go back to the room. Father is standing next to the dresser and Fatima is sitting on the edge of the bed. I dry my face with the towel hanging from the chair back. I start to take off my pyjama top, so I can put on trousers and a shirt. Father says: "Don't waste time. Just go in your pyjamas." He gives me half a franc. I say: "Where's the dish to put it in." Fatima answers: "On the sideboard."

I go out of the room but leave the door partially open. I take the dish. Father closes the door to the room. I open the front door and then slam it shut. I rush to hide under the table. I sneak under the side away from the door to the skylight, so that the tablecloth will cover me completely. My head bumps against the edge of the table. I put my hand over my mouth to keep from screaming. I rub on the bump. I stay clear of the cockroach nests piled up in the corners. My heart is pounding. I cannot get out of my hiding place to get any closer to the room. I listen carefully. Not a sound. I can't chance moving. My heart keeps beating hard. *The morning's light settles over the room. I enter quietly without the two of them sensing me. I hide behind the wooden post for the clothes line. I shrink up between my father's suit, his fly whisk, and his umbrella. I can hear them moving on the bed. The sound of muffled laughter. His or hers? On the nightstand next to the bed, a cup of water holds his false teeth. I pull his jacket to the side. His back is to me. On his bare head, light grey hair surrounds his bald spot.*

I can see the side of his smiling face. His arms surround mother. She's laughing too. I reach my hand out to his coat. I press on the inside pocket where he keeps his money. I take it all. I steal out of the room. They come out after a while. He goes back to the room. He calls me. He closes the door. Sits me in front of him. Questions me. He takes the bamboo cane from on top of the dresser. He beats me with it.

I hear movement. The door to the room opens. Fatima comes out. She moves between the sideboard and the kitchen. Her clogs clomp. She makes a plate of *ful* beans. She takes it to father and stays inside. After a while, she comes back out. She opens the front door and goes out, closing it behind her. Father comes out of the bedroom and goes to the bathroom. He mutters a few verses. I can tell he is doing ablutions. I crawl under the table in the direction of the front door. I can see his legs in front of the sink. I leave my hiding place, holding the dish. I go to the front door. Softly, I open it, then close it hard. Father is still at the sink. He rubs water over his ears. He turns to me and says: "Did Fatima forget to close the door?"

I say as I wave the empty dish at him: "The oil shop's closed. It's Friday."

He says: "They used to open for a while before high prayer. Shall I make you an egg?"

I say: "I'm not hungry." I go into the room and sit at my desk. I take the notebooks out of my satchel. I open my reading textbook. I read a poem called "Lament of a Cat." Father comes in. He spreads the prayer rug out on the floor and prays the morning prayer.

He puts on his clothes. He goes out to pray the high prayer at the mosque. I make sure that the doors to the apartment and the bedroom are both locked. I open the dresser. I drag the desk chair over in front of it. Climb up. On the front of the top drawer there's a glass pane with a picture of a lion. A bottle of Bislari's iron tonic. I take down *The Great Star of Knowledge*. I bring it to the desk. I flip through its pages. A little picture falls out of it, about the size of an I.D. photo. A new one. It shines. I can tell whose it is by the perfumed scent spilling off it. It is Tante Samira's. She looks just the way I saw her during Eid. Very beautiful.

I put the picture back in its place. I examine those pages that father has marked with slips of paper. I flip through the pages again. At the end of the book, there is an index of the four sections. I read through it quickly, making notes of important page numbers in my penmanship notebook. I start with page 108 in the first part. I don't understand a thing. I go to page 25 of the second part. Then page 61 of the third part, then 3 and 140 from the fourth part.

I read: "Take the skin of an owl and dye it with henna and alum, then write on it the letter aleph and draw next to it the name of the angel in cursive, the invocation and the ellipsis, make it into a cropped hood and wear it." What does "the ellipsis" or "a cropped hood" mean? I move on. "Write 'O Ko-reishite, Sharaibite, Yahoubite' on the sand, then sit on it and recite from the holy book, 'And we will make before them a wall,' along with the holy words, 'For they cannot see,' then say, 'Take their eyes and their sight and make them, O servant, these names in the sea wrapped in darkness that they might not see me. "Deaf are they and blind, For they cannot see."'"

I keep reading: "The divine benefits of the name 'Ghaffar.' Whosoever puts it inside a square during the last night of the month on a grey sheet of paper and carries it after reciting the name the same number of times as the day of the month, God will make him invisible to whosoever would do him harm." Next to this is a drawing of a square with four rows made from blocked off columns. The top of the columns are headed by the letters *gh, f, a,* and *r*. The other columns are marked by numbers.

I go back to "O Koreishite, Sharaibite, Yahoubite." I go to the few empty lines in the back of the penmanship notebook. I close the book and put both of them back in their place in the dresser, and push the chair back to its place.

I look out from the balcony. Abdel Hamid, the nutcase. He walks out of the building and heads toward the entrance to the alley. He is fully dressed and carrying a newspaper in his hand. *Mother forcefully presses the key into the lock. She pushes the door. I go into the room. She locks the door behind me with the key. My father stands at the window. He looks over the comings and goings in the street. I tell him about mother. A stone falls from the window. I hear one of the children chanting: "There goes the crazy man!"*

Father comes back in carrying a bag of grapes on the vine, with the plump fruit. And another of Armenian cucumbers. I don't like them when they have a bitter taste. I like the local ones better.

I wait until he has changed clothes. I pretend to be memorizing my daily Quranic verses. I ask him about the verse that starts off, "And we will make before them a wall." He knows most verses by heart. He finishes the verse for me.

Uncle Fahmi brings a round box of sweets over to us. On its cover, there is a full-color picture of a European boy wearing a tall cap and holding a cane. I take the box from him and put it on the desk. He sits on the edge of the bed. He wears a dark brown jacket and beige trousers. He is carrying a book. He puts it on the desk. Father sits cross-legged next to him. They turn to face each other. I sit at my desk. I go back to my review of grammar, syntax, meter, and pentameter. I grab Uncle Fahmi's book, *The New 1,001 Nights* by Abdel Rahman al-Khamissi. The Everyman's Book series. Five Piastres. Father warns me: "Leave the book alone and go back to your homework." I tell him I've finished going over all the grammar. He says: "Study something else then." He shouts at Fatima to make some coffee. I pull out my chemistry notebook. I read about how to separate sand from salt.

Uncle Fahmi takes off his fez and puts it next to him. He passes his hand over his hair. There is a ring of matted hair from where the edge of the fez rested. He says the whole country is in an uproar over the divorce between the king and Queen Farida, and that the students at the high school for girls marched in protest and chanted "Farida's left the brothel. She's sworn off all betrothal!"

Fatima brings in two cups of coffee on a tray. She puts them on the round table. She hangs around for a second, saying: "Something else for you now, Bey?" Father says: "No thanks." She leaves the room. They sip the coffee without talking. Father says to him: "What is that fancy shirt you have on?"

"Van Heusen." He takes a pack of Blair's no. 3 cigarettes out of his pocket.

Father asks him: "Did you switch?"

He says: "It's ten piastres cheaper than Three Fives brand." He offers one to father, but he turns it down, saying: "I never switch." Uncle Fahmi lights one with his Ronson lighter. I hand him the ashtray and he puts it between them on the bed. He asks: "Hey! Do you have a backgammon set?" Father shakes his head and says no. He says he used to play every night at "The Parliament," his regular coffeehouse, back in the days of the real estate trade. He sighs and begins to talk mistily about that time. The broker would walk from table to table with a map. He would throw a glance over at it and pick a piece of property. He didn't pay a cent. You could barely throw your dice or take a sip of your whisky before the broker would come back and announce he had sold your property for a good price. You would collect your profit without breaking a sweat. More than once, he would go back home in a horse-drawn cab with a purse full of gold coins in his hand.

He asks about Sameera. Uncle Fahmi answers that she's worried about Nadeen because she is so rebellious. She wants to go alone with her fiancé to the cinema. Father says: "So what?" He turns to me and I pretend to be absorbed in my reading. He goes on: "So what if they kiss each other or something? Doesn't she love him and plan on marrying him? Then that's that. You need to get over this old-timey talk. It's a new world."

Uncle Fahmi lights another cigarette. He says: "To tell the truth, Khalil Bey, I'm here about a personal matter." I lift my head up from the book and prick up my ears. Father turns toward me. I put my head back down. I start to move my lips and run the pen over the paper. Uncle Fahmi complains about Nabila wearing him out. He says: "I give her what she wants right away. I bought her an electric washing machine with a revolving element that holds 52 liters. I brought in a telephone line. I got an Electrolux fridge."

"Is it electric?"

"It works with oil, gas, or electricity."

Father asks "So what's she angry about?"

Uncle Fahmi leans his head towards father. I prick up my ears. Father turns towards me. He orders me to go study in the hall. I pick up my notebook and open up the door that has been left open a crack. I bump into Fatima who runs away quickly. I leave the door open a crack. I stand near it. Fatima stands in front of the sideboard. She makes herself busy filling the spice bins. I hear Uncle Fahmi say: "She doesn't want to sleep next to me, and she says I've lost my appetite for women."

Father says: "Is it true?"

"Listen, Khalil Bey. You understand what happens when a woman turns down her husband."

"What do you mean?"

Fahmi raises his voice in anger: "She's the one who killed my passion."

"Keep your voice down."

Fahmi goes on without paying attention: "I can't go on like this. I've been wearing these same clothes for a week. I can't change because all my clothes are back there." *We walk back and forth over the pavement in front of the Jewish school. The street is dark. Our apartment's lights are on. The bedroom window is open. We stop on the pavement in front of it. Mother and grandma are going through the dressers. They pull out clothes and pack up suitcases.*

Fatima and I look at each other. We listen and hear father's voice: "Where are you staying now?"

"At a friend's place. I can't go on like this."

"Okay. Don't panic."

"Now I'm just fine. I get up in the morning feeling just great."

He goes on talking in a low voice. Father's voice is direct: "That's just a morning cycle. It doesn't really mean anything." They stop talking. Father calls to me. I wait a second, then go in. He says: "Go get your English textbook. Show your Uncle Fahmi the words that you didn't know."

I drink a cup of cinnamon with milk. Fatima makes me the sandwich I'm going to take with me. Butter and strawberry jam. She wraps it in a sheet of newspaper and puts it next to the satchel on the desk. I put on my clothes and pick up the satchel, but I leave the sandwich. Father tells me to put on a sweater because it has turned cold. Father adjusts himself in his chair. He complains that his foot falls asleep. Fatima squats down on the floor and starts to rub his feet for him. I leave the room. I take out my key as I watch them from the corner of my eye. I put the key in my pocket and leave the door open a crack. I open the apartment door. I prick up my ears. No movement. My heart starts to pound. I shut the door with a bang and run under the table. I put the satchel in front of me. I hear the sound of the bedroom door closing. Father's voice: "Be sure to lock it." Fatima's voice: "I can't find the key." "Okay. It doesn't matter. Just come over here."

I raise my head, being careful not to hit it on the bottom of the table top. I open the satchel and take out the sand. I scatter it on the floor. I write on it with my finger: "O Koreishite, Sharaibite, Yahoubite." I sit on the sand. I keep a careful eye on the cockroach nests. I repeat in a soft voice: "Take their eyes and their sight and make them, O servant, these names in the sea wrapped in darkness that they might not see me. 'Deaf are they and blind, For they cannot see.'" Then I am quiet. I listen. No sound.

I come out carefully from under the table. I leave the satchel on top of the sideboard and go over to the door to the bedroom. My heart is pounding hard. I put my eye to the keyhole. I don't see anything. I turn my head and press my ear against it. I don't hear anything. I set my glasses back on the center of my nose. I gently turn the doorknob and push it just a little. I repeat to myself in my head: "O Koreishite, Sharaibite, Yahoubite." I take a step inside, confident that they won't be able to see me. Shining up at me is my father's bare bottom between the raised up, naked legs of Fatima. She is lying on the bed with her head down on the pillow. I take a step closer. I hear her say: "Oh well. It looks like you don't want it right now." He brings his mouth close to hers. She turns her mouth to the side. He tries to kiss her. She looks shocked. He tells her: "Open your mouth." She doesn't do it. He says: "Grab hold of it." She asks: "Like this?" He says: "Yes." After a second she says: "It's no use." I come closer. She turns toward me. She screams: "Holy shit!" She pushes him to the side and gathers up her clothes. She tries to sit up. Father turns his head. He shouts: "What the hell are you doing here?" I cry out: "Damn you both!"

I turn to leave the room. I snatch my satchel from the sideboard. I open the front door. Slam it hard behind me. I go out to the street and cross over to the other side. I walk along the narrow side street that runs parallel to the boulevard with the tramcar. I make it to school right at the end of the national anthem. I join in with the line as everyone heads up to the classrooms.

English class. Then natural sciences: properties of liquids, the theorem of Archimedes. We go down to the lab to do a chemistry experiment. The lab supervisor isn't there and the Bunsen burner doesn't work. The teacher uses the blackboard to explain extraction of oxygen from potassium chloride to us.

The bell for the short recess rings. The students get ready to go down to the playground. They all gather around Maher. His hair is parted from the left. His shirt collar is open and overlaps the collar of his suit coat. He is carrying some strange thing in his hand. He says it is not a camera, but a 3-D lens viewer. "Stereoscope videomaster." We have to work hard to repeat the name. He says that it grants its user the power, from its lens, to see the world as it really is. It shows 3-D pictures in natural color to make animals and surroundings clearer. The teacher comes over to us and puts out his hand to take the viewer. He looks into it and says: "Wow. It's as though the giraffe is standing right in front of you." Maher shows us the slot where you can load a card of slides. He says there are 94 cards and each one has seven full-color scenes. The teacher asks how much it costs. Maher is full of pride: "100 piastres."

"Wow. And the slides?"

"Twenty piastres each."

We go down to the playground. The school guard calls my name. He gives me a roll of paper, saying that a black man on a motorcycle brought it for me. The sandwich that I forgot. The children play with a ball made of socks. I watch them while I gulp down the sandwich. *We mark the two goals out with pieces of brick. We gather around Magdi and Hany. They flip a coin in the air. King or writing? Hany wins by taking king. He starts to choose the members of his team. He studies our faces. He points with his finger. The chosen one runs to his side, all proud. Magdi follows. My eyes meet his as he looks us over. His eyes keep moving and settle on the boy next to me. The choosing of the two teams goes on. I am the only one left. Each captain counts his team members. Magdi's team needs another player. As though surrendering, he waves me over.*

The bell rings announcing the end of recess. We go back up to class. The Arabic teacher comes in. He explains transitive verbs to us. He is stunned by how slow I am. A knock at the door. My heart starts to pound. The teacher calls out: "Enter." The geography teacher enters carrying a long cane. Standing behind him there is Lamae, he is good-looking with his thick lips and rosy face. The teacher steps over towards my desk, shaking his cane. His shoes are fat and bulging, like they're about to explode from both sides. My heartbeat get stronger, but he moves on past me and goes to the back rows where the older students and the ones who have been held back are sitting. He picks out one with a fat head. He drags him to the front of the class. He rains blows down on him with the cane without saying a word, then he calls him "ill-mannered" and "badly raised." The boy doesn't make a peep. He just takes the blows quietly. Then he settles back behind his desk. A loud silence settles over all of us. The Arabic teacher doesn't say anything. The geography teacher leaves. We start our lesson over again. We read out of our textbook a story called: "A

Strange Rescue From Certain Death." The teacher gives me a hard time for my mistakes in pronunciation.

The class ends. None of us say anything about what happened. We go down to the art classroom. The teacher is dark-skinned, medium height, and skinny. His necktie is loose. He's jumpy. He has a copy of the picture magazine *al-Musawwar* in his hand. He reads us the story of a thirteen-year-old boy from the magazine. "The boy tells his father, 'It's our shame that we stay here in Damascus while Palestine is burning. I'll get together a team of commandos from my friends, and we'll all get together in the town square.' The father admired his son's precocious manhood, so he kissed him and said, 'We'll go together, my son. And let the first volunteers in your team be your younger brothers.'"

He continues reading as he walks around the room: "The father joined the rescue operation forces and the son put together a team of thirty children. They snuck their way from the border all the way to Jerusalem. They attacked a Jewish stronghold in the King Dzavid section of the city. The youngest of them was infiltrating mine fields and setting them off. They almost took control of three houses that Jewish forces had held using assault rifles. They managed to blow up two of them. When the boy attacked the third, holding his rifle in one hand and a grenade in another, he shouted: 'You Haganah, if you're men, show your faces and fight me man to man.' No one dared come out, but a single bullet shot out and lodged in his back, killing him once and for all."

The teacher goes to the blackboard, and says: "Everyone

draw what you liked best from the story." I draw the father and his son. The picture doesn't seem very good to me. I erase the whole thing. I draw an open field with plants and trees. I try to figure out what mines look like and where I should put them. The teacher walks around behind us. He looks over what we draw. He leans over and draws me a tree. He pats me on the back to encourage me. I draw a boy at the edge of the field.

The teacher asks me and three others to stay after class. He takes us out to the school's garden. We sit down on a green grassy spot under some trees. He promises that he is going to turn us into artists. He tells us to draw a branch of a tree with all its leaves. I carefully trace the shape of the branch and the leaves with my pencil. I fill up the whole page. I go back over the lines with the ink pen. He says: "That's enough for today."

I take my satchel and leave the school. I go along the street that leads to the Jewish school. I walk along the colored gravel. I stop at the corner. I look to the left. The branches of the trees are bare. I step over red and yellow flowers. I make it to the pavement in front of our old house. The windows of our apartment are open. You can see somebody's shadow moving. A steamroller parks up a few steps ahead. A side of the road has been paved with asphalt. The smell of burning tar. *A pile of gravel is in front of the house. The stones shine in the moonlight. We stand on top of it. We rub stones together. Colored sparks come off them. My father calls me and I rush back inside. I go to the bathroom first. I wash my face and my feet. I go and find him at the window. The darkness is lifting. Mother is singing as she brings in coffee.*

I go back to where the street begins and from there to the square. I cross it, passing in front of Hajj Abdel 'Alim's shop. I go back into the alley. I see that father is standing on the balcony. The wide woolen scarf is wrapped around his neck. The big woolen cap covers his head. His neck is twisted towards the top of the alley. As soon as he sees me, he goes back in. I go up the stairs. I open the door with my key. I go into the room. He stands next to the wardrobe, holding the book *The Great Star of Knowledge*. He doesn't talk to me.

I put my satchel on the desk. I take out my notebooks. Stacks them up. I watch him from the corner of my eye. He turns around. He opens the book and lays it on the bed. He leaves the room. I steal a look through the crack in the door. I can hear him making dinner in the kitchen. I take the key to our room out of my pocket, and push it into the keyhole. I go over to the bed, and bend over the book. A small booklet is tucked inside its cover. I pick it up to read the name of it. I'm expecting something like "How to Punish an Abusive Child."

Full Male Potency. I flip through the pages, but I don't understand a thing, so I put it back in its place.

I go out to the hall. I am looking for him. There is no sign of him in the bathroom or the kitchen. I go back to the hall. The door to the skylight is closed. I go over to Mama Tahiya's room. The door is closed. I look through the keyhole. As it has been, without a piece of furniture. I go around the table. The door to the guest room is closed. I look through the keyhole. He is sitting on the couch facing me. His head is bowed and he is studying the floor. He raises his hands to his face. Suddenly, he breaks into tears and starts sobbing like a child.

He finishes praying the Friday prayer, on top of the bed. He goes back to his corner with a frown, sitting by himself next to the wall. The full-length prayer beads are in his hand. He sticks on the name "the Benevolent," repeating it.

I hear noise in the alley. I put on my glasses and rush to the balcony. He raises his voice, reciting the names of God without turning to me. His voice is like a warning not to make any noise.

I stop behind the glass pane. The children have paper kites. They're floating up in the air over the alley in all different sizes and colors. *He makes me an orange-colored kite. I go up to the roof of the house with the other children. Everyone has his own kite with him. We hold tight to the string. We throw them in the air. They fly up high.*

The children run underneath their hovering kites. They move out of my sight. I go back to the desk. I review the lesson on lengths of measure and use of the compass and ruler. The cry rings out in the alley: "Knife blades and scissors!" I rush back to the balcony. The man is in the middle of the alley behind his sharpener. Samir brings him a lot of knives. He pushes the wheel with his hand to get it spinning. He puts the edge of the blade against it. Sparks come flying off. He grips the handle and moves it sideways to its tip. He lifts it and puts the other side on the wheel. Abdel Hamid shows up, coming from the entrance to the alley. He walks along seriously until he gets to the door of the house. *We pass out of the big iron gate. My father clutches a bag of apples to his chest. We walk over a long, dusty path with dead trees on either side. We come to a one-story house. Nurses with huge bodies. One comes to us wearing a long metal chain around her waist. It drags behind her on the bare tiles. Her cracked sandals scrape against the floor. Their heels are striped with black cracks. A long hallway with rows of shut doors on both sides. Some of them have iron doorknobs. Behind them are women wearing strange looks. One of them laughs with loud peals of laughter. She points to a woman who is pale and fat with a face full of pimples, whispering: "Come here." I grab hold of my father's hand. An open hall with many beds. Mother is lying on one. She smiles quietly. My father holds the bag of apples out to her. She takes one of them. She wipes it off with her hand and nibbles at its side. She feels my face with her fingers. She asks me about school but doesn't seem to care. The huge nurse watches us from close by, keeping her eyes on the apples.*

His fingers make it to the middle beads on the string. I open the satchel. I get out the marbles that I still have. I am careful to keep all the same kind. Most of them are shaped like balls and are transparent with twisting stripes inside of all different colors. I pick out four that are different shapes and sizes. I put them to one side to change them during the game.

His fingers come close to the end of the string. I put the satchel to the side. I open the composition notebook. I write the word "Reading" in the middle of the line. I think, then I skip a line and write in big letters: "Reading and the Comprehension of the Reading." It fills up the line. I skip another one and go to the line after that. I stop because I can't think of what else to write.

I wait until he finishes the string. Unsure, I go close to him carrying the draft notebook and fountain pen. He always writes my compositions for me and then I put them in my own handwriting. I look up at his smooth-shaven cheek. He takes the notebook from me.

He says: "Hand me a pencil."

Author's acknowledgment

My thanks to the poet Hamza Qanawy for the help he offered in working with and reviewing the original Arabic manuscript at various stages.

Translator's acknowledgments and note

Sonallah Ibrahim was an engaged and insightful participant in this English version of his novel, and I thank him for his help. Thanks also to Mohamed Aboul-Ela, Richard Bartlett, Ayman El-Desouky, Sayyid Fathi, Jennifer Grotz, Ahmad Hassan, and Richard Jacquemond, each of whom helped me at various stages and in diverse ways. In translating quotations from the Quran, I have referred to Michael Sells, *Approaching the Qur'án: The Early Revelations,* Ashland, Oregon, 2001, and *Al-Qur'án: A Contemporary Translation,* by Ahmed Ali, Princeton, 1993.